AMNESIA BITES

(Shady Arcade Book One)

SHARON STEVENSON

To Mum

For always being there

ALSO BY
SHARON STEVENSON

Short works in the Raised series:
Walking Away (novella, coming soon)

The Shady Arcade Trilogy:
Amnesia Bites
Sweet Oblivion (coming soon)
Beyond Shadows (coming soon)

At Hell's Gates Anthologies:
At Hell's Gates: Existing Worlds
(Gallows short story: Welcome to Hell)
At Hell's Gates: Origins of Evil
(stand alone horror short: Forget Me Never)
At Hell's Gates: Bound by Blood
(stand alone horror short: Monster)

Saint's Grove Standalone Paranormal Romance:
Heart (Book 10 of 12)

All Saint's Grove Novels in Series Order:
Immortal Ties by Jennifer Malone Wright
Hearts Aligning by Miranda Hardy
Her Forbidden Knight by Carly Fall
Racing Time by Elizabeth Kirke
Crossing Time by M.H. Soars
Across the Universe by Elise Marion
The Ghost and the Belle by Rose Shababy
All Dragons' Eve by Casse NaRome
Worlds Apart by Amy Richie

Heart by Sharon Stevenson
Enchanted Souls by Tia Silverthorne Bach
Thy Heart's Desire by P.T. Macias

Forthcoming works:

The Gallows Novels, Raised and Shady Arcade series are all expected to be completed by the end of 2017. Release dates for the remaining books are still to be announced.

Sign up to Sharon's newsletter to be the first to know about release dates and new works:
http://sharonstevensonauthor.com/newsletter/

AMNESIA BITES

CHAPTER ONE

Zack poked at the hole between his left pinkie and his ring finger, filling up with dread as he realised it had widened considerably since the day before. The gloves were falling apart again, and he didn't like what that meant. Every time he repaired them, it took him days to get used to the weird tingling between his fingers. Better this than the alternative, though: buying a new pair.

He didn't mind the expense or the annoyance of finding the right fit for his long fingers, but the story they pushed through him was something else entirely. Someone somewhere left their mark on each and every little thing that was produced every day in every part of the world, and the gloves were no different. The problem was he'd get to discover who'd left their mark the second his bare hands touched them. They'd be infused with something he didn't want to experience, some measure of melancholy that wasn't his own but that would slip under his skin and force him to experience the dark emotions he tried so hard to avoid. The effect never fully wore off, so every time he put them on he'd get the same damned story played out in strong emotional resonances that felt like his own.

Eventually, this would fade into an echo of a feeling which would still absorb into his skin but would become a dull background noise. The worst part of the whole thing was no matter where he bought his clothes, the feelings they'd absorbed were always negative. They weren't typically made by workers who loved their jobs; sure, maybe the designer had been happy, but the production line staff were generally a tired, over-worked, miserable bunch who left their unhappiness in the end product without ever knowing it.

Well, Zack knew it, and it gave him a headache. He tried to count himself lucky that it was only his hands that would feel the pain—his body had no idea if his shirt and trousers were depressed—but that only made him more anxious about his current problem. New gloves were not happening.

He ignored the hole, which was easy to do since it wasn't in a place that would let his bare skin touch his desk. His unbearably lonely desk. He'd grown sick and tired of feeling sorry for the damned thing.

He straightened as his office door opened. Well, more of a back room than an office, but he was happy enough to make do since it was windowless and more peaceful than expected for a unit inside a rundown, small town shopping arcade.

The professionally dressed blonde who manned his reception desk on the shop floor stood in his doorway, one hand on her hip as she informed him that he had a client.

"Are you ready for company or should I tell him to wait?"

Bridget didn't bother to lower her voice as she spoke, her bored tone letting him know the 'client' was another one of those damned private school kids looking for a cheap way to have a laugh on his lunch-break. She had no patience for pleasantries. It was the cop in her. She was only playing receptionist, and she didn't seem to particularly enjoy it.

He cleared his throat. "I'm ready."

She nodded and stepped back from the doorway.

The boy who walked in had a pensively drawn frown that he threw back at Bridget as she closed the door. Zack caught the snide smile on her exquisitely pretty face before she disappeared from sight. The boy indeed wore the blue and grey uniform that signalled he went to the private school down by the lake. Less expectedly, he clutched a little pink purse.

Zack motioned for him to take a seat. "What can I do for you?"

"I heard you can find people."

He raised an eyebrow, a little shocked. This was usually the line adults who visited his agency gave, the ones actually looking to enlist the help of a licensed detective with alleged psychic abilities, not the snickering little brats who came to amuse themselves at the local freak show's expense. He'd built up a poker face for those moments and could usually keep it on until they pissed off back to their afternoon lessons. Sometimes, he even managed to get a laugh at their expense.

Shaking out of his thoughts and nodding slowly, he

wondered just how many fifteen-year-old boys carried purses around these days. Chances were high this wasn't a trend most likely to catch on.

"That's right. Usually, though…" He didn't quite know how to put it. His parlour trick price was substantially lower than his rate for actual detective work. One real job every month or so could keep him going for a while, but the freak show act made sure his funds between times never ran out. This kid didn't look like he was here for a laugh, but Zack doubted he had the cash for anything more substantial, even if his parents might.

He was proved right when the kid whacked a twenty down on the desk and put the purse down after it with considerably more effort. His knuckles had turned white while on the damn thing.

Zack gazed down at it, imagining how happy it *should* feel, given the bright colour and pretty little bow. Dread flooded through him as he looked at it, not quite ready to remove his gloves.

"That's the rate for one question," he said, not wanting to give him any false hope.

"I know," the kid said, face scrunched up with determination underneath his pallor. "It should be enough."

At least, he didn't seem to be expecting more than he could pay for. Sighing inwardly, Zack removed his right glove. Hope glowed in the kid's eyes as he watched Zack touch the purse.

The trace feelings of desperation he picked up instantly were overshadowed by the terror that engulfed him, making him jerk back in his chair and curse loudly, right before the vision flooded his brain.

This happened once someone had owned an object for long enough. It became theirs, saturated with their thoughts and memories imprinting themselves over the original production-line-embedded feelings. The kid hadn't just bought this thing, after all; it had belonged to someone. None of that worried him. It was the intense fear that grabbed hold and swept through him that was making him shake now, causing his heart to race and his mouth to dry up. Something terrible had happened to the owner of this purse. Something he was about to bear witness to.

Zack hit the button to call Bridget back in before the room itself faded in front of him, giving way to an open air car park in the middle of night.

The broken remnants of a street lamp at his feet appeared to be thickly coated with a dark substance he didn't want to identify.

A shriek cut through the stillness, and he turned to see a young woman with long dark hair fall down in front of him, the whoosh of air as her body hit the ground making him shudder uncontrollably. Blood obscured the left side of her face, her dark eyes empty and staring.

The sound of an engine behind him let him know the girl's attacker was getting away. He moved quickly, pushing the horror of what he'd just witnessed down. The dark estate car was gone before he could get more than a few rushed steps closer. The part of the licence plate he'd seen, he repeated to himself over and over again, knowing that when the vision cleared, he'd find it almost impossible to remember otherwise.

As light slowly replaced the darkness around him, he studied the details he'd been given. The girl wore a pink T-shirt and bleached jeans. She had dark hair and eyes, just like the kid who'd brought him the purse.

Reciting the partial licence number, he closed his eyes.

When he opened them again, he was back in his office sitting behind his desk with one hand on the purse. The kid was staring at him open-mouthed.

He ignored the weird look and muttered the licence numbers under his breath until he had them written down. It could be difficult to write with gloves on, but he'd taught himself to do it so that he'd never have to put up with the emptiness the average ballpoint had buried within it.

"What was that?" the kid asked, sounding awestruck.

A horror story in extreme close up for me, kid. A glimpse at the freak show your friends told you about.

He shook his head and pulled his poker face back on. His job was almost done here. He could forget this shit soon enough.

"Who does this belong to?"

He was almost afraid to ask. Holding back a shudder, he removed his hand from the purse and put his glove back on. The cutesy pink thing appeared evil to him now, mocking him from the desk in its own unique, inanimate way.

He grabbed the purse, thankfully taking it out of Zack's sight. "My sister. Can I ask my question now?"

Bridget made them both jump as she opened the office

door and looked questioningly at Zack. "What's wrong?"

"Maybe nothing. Stick around." Code for *don't leave me alone right now.*

She nodded, coming into the room and closing the door. She sat primly behind the client, brushing at the leg of her grey trouser suit. Her clear blue eyes never left Zack's face.

He relaxed slightly. "Where did you get the purse, kid?"

"My name's Dorian," he said, sounding thoroughly insulted at being called a kid.

Zack rolled his eyes, making Bridget smile. "Where did you get this, Dorian?"

Dorian picked it back up. "It's my sister's. It was next to her car."

The bags under his eyes should have tipped Zack off in the first place. He should have told him to leave the minute he came in. He'd never get the sight of that girl falling down dead at his feet out of his head now. She'd haunt him for weeks. Those dark, vacant eyes, and that blood flowing from her cracked skull… touching the purse had been a mistake.

He ground his teeth as he tried to calm himself down. It wasn't working, but he couldn't stand to finger-tap pulse points in front of people. The weird looks that got him only stressed him out more. He concentrated on his breathing instead.

Bridget got to her feet and placed a hand on the kid's shoulder, and her voice hardened when she spoke. "What's going on here exactly?"

"I need to know," the kid said, his voice getting louder. "I need to know who killed my sister."

The determination on his face shot right through Zack, jolting him into action.

He lifted his mobile phone out of his pocket and turned away from them both. "Excuse me a moment. I have to take this call."

***

Bridget sighed as Zack turned his chair around to face the wall. She dropped her hand from the kid as he glanced at her again, clearly confused at what the man he'd asked to help him was doing.

"Steve, I've lost… I'm losing it again," Zack said, grabbing at his hair with his gloved hand.

She bit her lip, gauging the situation and waiting to figure out what to do with the kid. Zack was going into melt-down mode, and she needed to know what the hell had caused it. But she couldn't walk the brat out of there and find out how badly Zack was cracking up at the same time.

Zack's chair creaked slightly to the right. His voice took on a soothing lilt. "Calm down, Zack. Everything's just fine. Relax. Listen, I'm sure it's not as bad as you think it is."

She winced. He'd gone straight into 'Steve', his invented therapist. His speech had slowed, and he spoke quietly. She'd been hoping the guy would turn out to be real and that Zack had actually dialled his number, but apparently, the phone was a prop right now. What a bizarre thing to see happen, and this was only about the tenth time she'd actually witnessed it in the six months she'd been watching over him. Something messed up had to have happened, something that had poked at his trauma.

He laughed maniacally as his chair swung back slightly to the left. He became his own hysterical self again. "How can you even say that? Another girl is dead. They're still out there! They're real, and they're still out there. I thought they were gone, but no…"

She cringed hearing those words. Exactly what they didn't need. This was going to be a bad one. The boy was staring goggle-eyed at the man she was paid to protect. This situation had trouble written all over it.

"Right, come on, get up," she muttered, giving his shoulder a shove.

"What?" Dorian wasn't moving. "No chance. I need his help…"

"Who are you talking about, Zack?" Steve's soft voice returned as Zack's chair moved swiftly to the right again. "You're talking crazy. Is this the monsters thing again? I think you know 'they' don't exist." He paused. "There is no dead girl, is there?"

Zack's self-doubt appeared when he moved to the left once more. "I… I thought there was. I saw her, I'm sure… I mean I think."

Steve was quick to wrestle control at the first sign of Zack's doubt. The smooth swing to the right came before his typically reassuring comments. "It's all right, Zack. You're simply seeing things again. All you need to do is take your tablets."

Zack sighed as he swung back lazily to the left. "Goddamn it! I'm not seeing things."

His tone had lost all of its punch. He sighed again, pulling at his hair hopelessly.

Steve ended the conversation, as always, with the simple but firm statement, "Take your pills."

Zack's chair stopped moving as he took the phone away from his ear. Bridget watched the kid; he merely blinked as Zack turned back around, clasping his gloved hands in front of him, no trace of crazy in his dark brown eyes.

"Where were we?"

"He was just leaving," she said, the warning tone in her voice directed at the brat.

"I was not," Dorian protested.

She frowned at him. If she were in a less preoccupied mood, she might have forced the issue. As it was, her attention was split over Zack's melt-down and what it could mean.

Zack took a breath. "Your sister is dead. When did this happen?"

He swallowed audibly before he talked. "Last week. Friday night. She was supposed to be going to see a film, but she never came home."

Bridget watched Zack carefully as he took in that information. If he attempted another call to his imaginary therapist, she was calling time on the whole mess and getting rid of the boy before he could cause any trouble for them.

"And the police don't have any leads as to who killed her?"

He appeared remarkably calm by now. She couldn't help but wonder if he'd imagined taking his imaginary medication.

The kid shook his head. "I don't have the money to hire

you properly, but I thought if I paid you for the answer, then I could check the guy out myself."

Ballsy. Stupid, too, but she had to give him some props for his gutsy attitude.

Zack shook his head.

"I can't tell you who killed her. The guy got away too fast." He pulled a scrap of paper off of his writing pad and passed it to the kid. "Here. That's part of his licence plate number. You could give that to the police. Might help."

The brat picked it up along with the purse. The disappointment on his face made his features sag.

"I thought…"

"I'm not a miracle worker, kid," Zack said.

Dorian stared at his gloved hands as he got up. "Okay. Thanks."

Bridget opened the door, and the kid left. She closed it again and locked eyes with Zack. "You did it again."

His face flushed. "It?"

She nodded. "Steve."

He broke his gaze, dropping it to the table. She drank in the sweet smell of him as long as he was distracted, longing stirring deep within her. Strong emotions, particularly the negative kind, always seemed to make the scent of a human much more tantalising. She hadn't been this tempted by anyone in a while. Pinching her arm, she tore her focus back and told herself he couldn't possibly taste anywhere near as good as she imagined.

"It must have been because of the vision," he finally said, tonelessly. "The girl fell down dead right at my side. She was so young."

"How young?" She'd found it easiest to ground him with questions based around facts.

"I don't know. A little bit older than the boy."

Time for the reality check. "And you think you could have done something to help her?"

He shook his head, ruffling his overgrown dark brown hair with one of his leather-gloved hands. "No."

"Then stop worrying about it."

It should have been the end of things, but if Bridget knew Zack—and she definitely did—this wasn't the end. Not by a long shot.

He sighed. "Is lunch here yet?"

Her smile tightened. 'Lunch' always made everything better, didn't it? She had to fight not to roll her eyes at him as she opened the door. "I'll check."

CHAPTER TWO

The sandwich bitch made her deliveries between one and two every day, and every day Zack ordered a ham and cheese sub roll with mayo and pepper. That meant every day, Bridget had to stare down her worst nightmare in the perfectly toned flesh.

She heard the clacking of the woman's summery clogs on the tiled floor outside before her tartily packaged body appeared in their doorway. Bridget folded her arms. If Zack wasn't such a quaking mess around women, she'd have snatched the sandwich from her before she could even get the chance to clop into the office and ask about him. She tried to relax. Cassandra probably didn't present a real danger to him, but Bridget didn't like to take chances when the stakes were so high. A nuisance at best, she'd rather the woman didn't get the chance to become anything more than a passing fancy to the man she was being paid to protect.

Shaking her head, she put on her best coldly condescending smile. "Cassandra. You're looking… pink today."

The woman shrugged, grinning inanely. "Rico got new stock in. He wouldn't let me leave without taking one in every colour. How's Zack? Is he in?"

The dress was more suited to a night clubber. At least Cassandra had the decency to wear it with jeans even if they looked like they'd been painted on.

Bridget shook her head slowly. "He doesn't want to be disturbed."

"Oh, okay," she said, face falling for a fraction of a second before it picked back up into full-on beam.

Bridget picked up her ceramic coffee container. "If you don't mind, we're busy today."

The woman put the sandwich down on Bridget's desk. The bag barely contained the full god-awful thing, and it all stank of vinegar and dead pig. Bridget screwed her nose up.

Cassandra left, knowing better than to ask if Bridget wasn't going to start ordering her own lunch from her shop. Never in a million years, even if she did eat solid food.

She picked the monstrosity up and knocked on Zack's door before she opened it. He had his head cocked to one side and was nodding. Sighing inwardly, she placed the sandwich on his desk and folded her arms. "Are you okay, Zack?"

He frowned and nodded again. "I know. I love you, too. Speak to you later… Oh, and stop having weird premonitions about me, okay? Bye." He sighed as he locked eyes with Bridget. "Sorry, she can talk for Britain."

"She?"

What the hell? This was a new one on her. Had his

condition worsened? Should she report it to her superiors? Rick was not going to be happy if he was losing his shit on her watch. She folded her arms and braced for his answer.

"Audrey," he said as if the name should mean something to her. He pulled his wrapped sandwich over, not noticing her strange stare. "Her phone bill must be *huge.*"

"You weren't on your phone," she told him, raising an eyebrow.

He laughed at her.

"Good one. Ah," he said, taking his gloves off and flexing his fingers. "Ooh, yeah." He glanced up. "Do you mind? I'd like to be alone with my sandwich."

Sighing, she shrugged and left him to it.

***

The sandwich tasted like pure sunshine wrapped in pleasure-soaked joyousness. He sighed happily after his first swallowed bite. For Zack, food often had no taste. Whenever he could, he took home-made options because that was the only way it had any chance of tasting good for him. Cassandra's food was always lovingly prepared, and he appreciated every single amazing bite.

Moaning at the second bite, he heard a crash in the other room and hesitantly put the sandwich down. Getting up, he moved around the desk quickly, very nearly forgetting to protect his hands from the angry doorknob.

As he yanked his gloves on, he heard Bridget cursing under her breath. He was always surprised at just how spicy certain situations turned her language. She knew a lot of words he'd barely even heard of. She'd told him it was a cop thing the one time he'd been shocked enough to comment on it. Spend your life dealing with the scum of the earth and you end up learning new words to describe their awfulness. He didn't even want to know what she did usually at work. Though it was clear this largely uneventful bodyguard work was taking its toll on her patience.

"Is everything—"

He found her crouched on the floor, mopping up a broken mug. No, wait; that was her coffee container. The contents had splashed across the floor, and for a second he thought he was having a flashback to the vision that had shown him the dead girl.

"What is that?"

He crouched beside her. The bright spot of red on her hand took away any doubt he might have had about what had been in her cup. He shivered. It couldn't be real. He was clearly seeing things. He had to be. The vision had affected him more than he'd even realised.

Blinking, he stood back up and stopped staring at the scarlet liquid he couldn't explain. "Never mind."

"It's a diet mix," she said, sighing as she cleaned it up, ditching paper towels and the remnants of her mug in the bin under her desk. "Honey and tomato juice."

"Maybe you should just go and get a sandwich," he suggested, thinking back to the one he'd just abandoned on his desk. He felt himself relax almost instantly. Lunch was a much safer thing to think about. Even if there was a reason for the colour of Bridget's drink to resemble blood, it was still creepy as hell and reminded him too much of his vision.

"Maybe," she said, sounding non-committal.

"Carbs aren't so bad," he muttered, his attention splitting.

"Yeah, sure. Get back to your sandwich."

He headed back into his office, closing the door behind him. The food wasn't quite the same when he got back to it. It still had that sunshine-y taste, but something less pleasant had tainted it. *The desk*, he thought, damning the stupid thing to hell. If Bridget's desk hadn't been used so sordidly by its previous owner, he'd have asked her to swap with him. Lonely was a bit less annoying than sexually aroused, so he settled for a half depressed sandwich and told himself he'd never leave one of Cassandra's creations alone with it ever again.

CHAPTER THREE

Bridget waited. She was used to waiting, but it still bored the utter shit out of her. She researched vacation options on her laptop, ignoring the fact that she wouldn't be getting the chance at a holiday anytime soon. Her job was more than full time. It was more than a job, even; it was her life. *Zack* was her life. She should be just thrilled. Too bad babysitting a mentally unstable man-child was not on her list of reasons for existing.

It's just a job. She'd keep repeating that to herself until it was all over.

As she clacked away at the keyboard, hunger pangs rose, twisting her stomach in their vise. Lunch had been ruined, and now all she could think about was eating. Typical. Not as if she could walk along to the sandwich shop and ask them nicely to cater to her special dietary requirement. She seriously doubted Cassandra would happily hand over two pints of what Bridget was craving.

She glanced at Zack's door. He'd go home soon and then she could call her boss. Rick hadn't gotten back to her yet, and she'd marked her email urgent. Chances were he was out. He never had figured out how to sync his emails with his phone. She tapped her nails off the desk. They were looking ragged lately; no time to get them manicured, and she'd never gotten the hang of doing them herself.

By the time Zack's door opened, she was ravenously contemplating going out for an illegally obtained snack before she even bothered to call Rick. Chances were she wouldn't get the time once the big boss man started ordering her around.

"'Night, Zack."

He nodded and left, head down, movements swift. She got up when she was sure he'd gone, opening the door and sniffing at the air. Larry, the security guard, was still around. He wouldn't be her first choice; the combination of greasy skin and dandruff tended to put her off, but beggars had a hard time being choosers, and it wouldn't be the first time she'd considered him. Oh, but a slightly more tempting offer was walking her way, and she smiled at her good fortune, wondering if the girl would even see it coming.

She wore her usual weirdo punky clothes, today comprising of a tight blue and black tartan vest over a black leather skirt and fishnet tights. Her shoulder bag was adorned with little pewter skulls. *How cute.*

"Chloe, how nice to see you."

The girl looked up past her long dark fringe and scowled. "Bite me, bitch."

"If you insist," Bridget murmured, smiling at the thought of sinking her teeth into Chloe's pale throat.

Her vision blurred as she became overcome with blood-lust until all she could see was the precious vein bulging in the girl's throat, ready and waiting to release sweet blood into Bridget's mouth.

***

Chloe's eyes widened as Bridget took a step towards her. "Shit."

She shook her head, snapping out of her reverie.

"Get back, foul creature," she commanded, locking her gaze on Bridget and forcing her back into the shop with the power of her will, one that worked through a kind of magic that existed in her blood.

Chloe was a necromancer, a human with power to control the dead. As a vampire, Bridget proved fair game, and right now she was shuddering uncontrollably as she obeyed Chloe's commands. She didn't dare break eye contact until she'd talked Bridget into Zack's office and locked the door on her.

"Shit," she swore again, leaning against the door and knowing she couldn't just leave a hungry vampire in a locked room. She rushed to the shop door and went back into the lobby, biting at her nails as she surveyed her options. Too late to leave and come back.

Larry was getting ready to lock up, swinging the keys in his hand as he whistled his way tunelessly around the lobby.

"Hey, Larry," she said when he came into view, getting ready to work her charms on him.

He wasn't a vampire, but he was a horny teenage boy,

and that was the other thing she knew how to order around when she needed to. She managed to force a pretty smile as he stopped jangling the keys and gave her a once over that lingered a little too long on her hemline.

"Can you help me out with those keys of yours? I left something in Zack's office."

Larry's gaze moved upwards. She found herself wondering if she was losing her touch; realising she was getting kind of close to thirty now, was that the age when her sex appeal might start to wane?

Finally, he nodded, flipping through the keys on his chain as she stepped back to let him in.

"So what did you leave?"

She froze. Half a dozen dumb answers went flying through her head all at once.

"My pen," she said quickly, glad she'd settled on something likely to actually be found in an office. 'My baby elephant' or 'the broken remains of my heart' might have seemed dubious in comparison. She damned the Discovery Channel for that first thought and decided to ignore the second entirely. "I was in the middle of writing something and if I switch to another pen, the ink might not match."

Larry put the key in the lock, glancing at her and, she was sure, her legs again. "Hey, are you doing anything on Friday night?"

She winced. "Uh, yeah…"

The door swung inwards, and Bridget flung herself at Larry. Chloe sighed as he shrieked. The tall, blonde vampire pinned him on the floor, straddling him. Her irises had gone completely black. She stared into his eyes until he closed them. He was all hers now.

Chloe grimaced as Bridget crunched down into Larry's long neck. Bridget's uncontrollable hunger had to mean she'd skipped a meal. She tried not to watch as the vampire sucked on her hormonally rife friend. From her angle, it looked like they were making out.

Shivering, she went to the shop door and kept an eye out. No one else was around. In another few minutes, the lights in the lobby would go off with no one around to trigger the sensors. Larry would have locked the exits now that all the customers had left, so they weren't in any danger of being disturbed. She stared into the lobby, trying to ignore the creepy sounds Bridget was making extracting Larry's blood.

Once the lights went out, she closed the door and swiftly walked over to the vampire.

"Stop eating. Get off of him. You're done."

Bridget followed her instructions slowly, hesitating and shaking as she moved off her unconscious meal and stood back. Chloe told her to stay still while she checked Larry was okay. He was breathing, and his pulse was steady. The tent he'd pitched in his pants showed her he wasn't too short on blood. She straightened up, wiping her fingers on the bottom of her vest. She watched Bridget as the blonde woman's eyes returned to normal. Her cheeks were flushed now as she glanced at Larry and winced.

"What happened?"

"You could have killed someone, that's what happened."

Chloe sounded pissed because she was. She hated

vampires. It didn't matter how civilised they tried to act—one missed meal was all it took to make their instincts take over. They were killers, and they didn't know how to change that; they could only try to suppress it.

"It won't happen again," Bridget said.

"If it does, you know what I'll do." She bent to help Larry up as he groaned.

"What the hell just happened?" He dropped his keys as he stumbled to his feet.

Chloe grabbed them, not caring that she'd likely just flashed her underwear. The poor guy had come this close to being sucked dry by a stupid walking-corpse.

She frowned at Bridget. "I'm watching you."

Bridget folded her arms. "I've got nothing to hide."

"Get your stuff. We're leaving."

The woman's jaw slackened for a second.

Chloe frowned at her. "What? It's not like the sun's still out."

"It's raining," Larry said, sounding dazed.

Chloe nodded, taking Larry's arm and not letting her eyes drop from Bridget as she moved past them at a quickened pace. She blew out a breath, but her heart was hammering. She'd just let a vampire drink directly from a human. If the necromancer's Council ever found out, she'd be toast.

Larry's head brushed her shoulder, and she snapped out of the thoughts that were starting to freak her out. She took a deep breath. She'd done what she had to do. Bridget had let her hunger get out of control. Nothing less than a controlled feed from a vein would have sated her—animal blood would have only made her crave human more violently—and there was nothing that would have made Chloe risk Zack's safety like that.

"Are we going out now?"

Larry sounded dazed, and he looked wasted. He needed to rest and she knew it.

Chloe sighed. "No. We're taking you home because you need to eat something and you need to sleep."

As if things weren't bad enough, she had to walk the guy home to make sure he didn't decide to go for a sleep in the rain. She doubted worse could happen to him than what already had, but still. He was kind of her responsibility right now.

Shaking her head, she tugged on his arm, and they started to walk out of Zack's agency and into the corridor. Bridget was waiting to be let out at the entrance to the arcade, scowling and kicking her pointed-toed-stiletto-clad foot against the bottom of the doors.

"Come on, Larry. Give me the keys, and let's get the hell out of here."

CHAPTER FOUR

The over-cast sky made it more pleasant for Bridget to walk home while the sun was still up. The summer nights always proved more awkward, but she'd chosen the apartment building close to the arcade on purpose. If worst came to worst, she was only ever twelve steps away from the place where she worked. Even a newly hatched vamp could manage less than sixty seconds in the sun.

She threw her bag onto the phone table and locked the door behind her. Her four little darlings gathered around her instantly, mewling and purring against her legs. The grey Persian cats were housebound and addicted to the taste of her blood. They were originally intended to be a source of food for emergencies only, but she'd grown so attached to them, they'd become familiars instead. To a witch, that might mean something different. To her, it meant she could see through their eyes whenever she fed them a drop of her blood. Blood magic was something a witch could use, but it remained primarily connected to vampires.

"Another boring day, my darlings," she told them,

picking up the king cat who stole most of the others' food and was hands down her favourite. He was a big round ball of fur in her arms, saving his ferocious hissing for when the other kitties attempted to get in his way. "Home at last, Arthur."

She went to the couch and sat down, rubbing Arthur's belly. She had slipped her phone into her pocket and she took it out now. The three neglected kitties mewled at her feet, the skinniest stretching and putting his paws on her knee.

"Down, Lancelot," she warned, right before Arthur hissed and reached out to scratch his brother.

The three cats at her feet dashed away quickly, and she was left with a pleasantly purring king cat on her lap, settling in and closing his eyes.

She called Rick, knowing the conversation would be rough.

He took his time answering, probably bemoaning the fact that this was outside the nine to five part of the job he was obligated to perform.

"Bridget," he said, sounding wary. "I wasn't expecting to hear from you. Is everything…okay?"

"You didn't get my message?"

"I couldn't get into my emails."

"Uh-huh. Well, do you really want to have this conversation over the phone?"

He sighed. "I don't have time to get into town."

"Okay, then. He's getting worse."

"In what way?"

"The episodes," she said, speaking in that slow, measured way she knew drove her boss nuts. "You know, those crazy little things he does ever since—"

"I get it," he snapped. "This is not good."

"Tell me about it."

"It's been six months," Rick said, a clicking noise travelling down the line.

She pictured him tapping his pen on his ink-blotter. He was still at work, then. Can't get to his emails—bullshit. Her smile turned into a grimace as she figured out what he was going to say next. It was inevitable, and the reason she'd ignored his last few episodes. That new one cinched it, though; Zack was deteriorating. They had to move fast.

"I'm aware of that."

"You think you've got the situation under control?"

"For now," she said, wondering what was holding Rick back.

"Okay, good."

"That's it?"

If that was all he had to say, she could breathe a heavy sigh of relief, for now.

"I'll be in touch."

He was going to speak to the higher ups, then.

The line disconnected, and she put her phone down on the arm of the seat. She got the feeling her metal was about to be tested, and she'd better damn well be prepared.

She ran her fingers through Arthur's thick fur. "I'll be ready."

CHAPTER FIVE

Zack relaxed into the bubble-filled hot water. He'd gone to a lot of trouble to find lovingly home-made bath products so that he could properly chill out at the end of those particularly stressful days. Days like today, when he'd seen a girl drop down dead inches away from where he stood.

Shivering, he took his gloves off and sat them on the soap rack in front of him, next to the tub of Cassandra's cherry ice-cream. The bath felt amazing enough to take the edge off and make him smile. The ice-cream was to keep the feeling going. He fully expected to be in the bath long enough to wrinkle every sliver of skin from his neck down to his toes. In half an hour, the ice-cream would be melted to perfection.

This was what he needed right now—a head full of happiness. No single diverted thoughts. He didn't need to think about that poor kid from the morning or the horrific thing that had happened to his big sister. That sounded like a job for the police.

He sighed blissfully as he fully submerged himself. The warmth encased him, soothing his worries away. Nothing was going to ruin his happiness. Nothing.

"Jesus, Zack, this denial shit again?"

Audrey's intruding voice invaded his happiness.

Why did he pick up the goddamned phone?

He groaned. "Damn it, Audrey, go away."

He'd had about enough of her warnings for one day.

"Look, you can't ignore me this time, and I know you're trying to."

She was right. "I'm not taking that case, so there's nothing to worry about."

"You don't take it. It's taking you. You never listen, do you?"

"If I promise to listen, will you stop talking?"

She laughed. Her laughter had a hiccupy sound to it, which he found highly irritating.

"That dead girl needs you," she said, sounding serious. "You'll figure that out soon enough. Something's off about this one, though. Something stinks. You have to be careful."

"Okay, okay," he said, gazing at the ice-cream. "I need to go."

"Promise me you'll be careful."

"I don't know what that means."

"Just… don't trust anyone."

He snorted. His paranoid sister telling him to trust no one; that was new. "Okay, whatever. Good night."

She stopped bothering him with her insane warnings, and he pulled the soap rack over to start in on his ice-cream. His night of relaxation was back on.

CHAPTER SIX

Bridget got to work early as usual, entering with the cleaning crew just before sun-up. The strange hours she kept to appear human had taken some getting used to, but she'd eventually tuned her body to it, like so many of her kind.

She put her ceramic coffee container down on the warming coaster and switched the device on. Powering up her computer, she wondered when her new orders would come in. Had Rick gone to his superiors yet or was he holding off?

She tapped her fingers on the desk as she waited for her computer to come on. Zack had been her life for so long. She found it hard to imagine that coming to an end. What had things even been like before? She had a problem with long-term memories. As soon as she'd become a vampire, she'd started to live in the moment. As a species, their synapses worked differently. Anything beyond six months was impossible to recall.

But, it wasn't important. She had files she could pull out if she really wanted to dig into the past. It was just sort of ironic, considering her current job.

That skinny, jittery life she currently didn't know how she was going to move on from made his entrance at nine a.m., throwing her a wan smile as he walked into his office and closed the door. He didn't remember anything beyond the last six months, either, but for totally different reasons.

She bit at her lip. An email came into her inbox, and she quickly opened it.

Rick's misspelled mess of a message wasn't quite the mission she'd been expecting, and disbelief rolled through her.

"What the..." she said, reading through it a second time to be doubly sure.

He was asking her to start Phase Two of Plan B. She didn't get it. Surely, Plan A made more sense. Plan B was riskier; it involved telling Zack things he didn't need to know.

But if he'd said it, that meant orders. She'd follow along.

She stared at the message before she hit delete. Plan B, it was.

CHAPTER SEVEN

Zack considered the situation from all angles as he walked around his desk. The possible locations of the girl's murder were few and within easy distance to check into. An outdoor car park that large… there were three possibilities, and he could eliminate one of those instantly. He would already have heard about the murder if it had happened in the parking lot at the back of the arcade. Plus, he probably would have picked something up when he walked past it. Incidents that left a vivid psychic imprint like that couldn't be ignored. If he'd been to where it had happened, he'd have known, regardless of how protected his skin was.

He clasped his hands together. He'd need to be prepared for it. He'd know the place when he found it, but it came with the problem that *he'd know it when he found it*. He couldn't go alone. Considering how frequently he had blackouts after a vision, he couldn't risk that.

He stopped walking in a circle and looked up at the closed door. It wasn't a case he could take to earn money. The kid didn't have any. Bridget would probably sigh and tell him they couldn't close the office for the day when he wasn't going out on a paying job. Then again, she was basically his body guard. Didn't she kind of have to do what he told her?

Hesitating, he folded his arms and leant back against his desk. He'd been fuzzy on the dynamics of their relationship ever since they'd been introduced. Awakening from a coma and being told he had to go into witness protection had been a shock. He remembered nothing of what he'd 'witnessed', but that didn't matter, of course. Someone dangerous out there knew he was alive, and that was enough to convince the police to assign him permanent protection. Bridget was day-watch. She alternated between bossing him around and playing obedient secretary. It made her kind of hard to approach.

He opened the door and closed it behind him once his feet were firmly planted in the front shop. The windows had been painted over, the only light coming through the glass-fronted door.

Bridget looked up, putting her coffee container down and leaning back in her seat. She eyed him suspiciously as he stood there working his way up to revealing his plans.

"Are you all right, Zack?" She narrowed her eyes slightly.

"There's something I need to do," he said, trying to sound sure about it.

She took a noisy breath and pushed her chair back from her desk. "The dead girl?"

How did she know?

She always just seemed to know. He nodded.

"What were you thinking?" she asked in her matter of fact voice, not the more sarcastic tone she sometimes brought out when she was trying to boss him around. She was at least willing to hear him out.

"I want to find the place," he said. "Maybe—"

She held up a hand, reaching over to click her mouse. The printer on the filing cabinet behind her started up seconds later.

"Got it," she said. "Looked it up last night."

She passed him the piece of paper. He peered down at the address. The college car park in town.

"I want to go and see if there's anything…else."

He winced at the thought of seeing it again, but it would be the best way to start off. He needed a second vision, one that would tell him who had killed the girl.

"We can go later," she said, sitting back down and beginning to clack away at her keyboard. She'd told him she still consulted on homicide cases while she was on 'baby-sitting duty,' as she liked to call it, so he supposed he shouldn't be so surprised that she'd looked into this already. "I'm pulling up her case file."

"Oh, that's… thanks." He went back into his office and continued walking around the desk.

***

The dead girl was Pauline McAllister, eighteen years old, and her parents had reported her missing a week past on Sunday.

Bridget tapped her nails on the desk as she surveyed the details. The girl was of age, physically fit, and had just moved out of her parents' house. She'd seen enough cases like it to be suspicious, but she'd need to play this safe.

Opening her emails, she started composing one to Rick. Her fingers paused over the keyboard. Was it really the best idea to drag him in so soon? A false alarm would only piss off the higher ups.

She deleted the message. She'd wait.

She could practically see Zack wearing down the floorboards in his office; the creaking her enhanced hearing picked up steady and predictable. He was likely pacing in a circle around his desk and would continue to do so until they picked up a client or she told him it was time to check out the car park.

She picked up her cup and drank the lukewarm blood like it wasn't decidedly unsatisfying after her fresh-from-the-veins meal the night before. She put the cup down when it was empty, catching sight of Larry on his rounds through the glass-panelled door. He threw her a smile in passing, and she licked her lips without realising it. Hunger washed over her. She was starving.

Blinking, she calmed herself. It would pass. She'd experienced this before. The handful of times she'd lost control and bitten a human, her eating habits had taken weeks to get back to normal. The animal blood she was supplied by the FBU—the Federal Bureau of the Undead, aka the vampire police force—was going to be unappetising for a while, but she'd get used to it again, eventually. She'd just have to nip home in a few hours and refill her cup before she headed out with Zack later.

***

Chloe sat behind the desk of her photo-shop lab, tapping a pen off a notepad. She sold alternative jewellery, indie rock CDs, and she offered photo-shop services, the most popular of which involved zombifying teenagers. Suffice it to say, her shop had a kind of limited clientele. Kids from the high school would pack the place at lunch-time, but right now, it was quiet and quiet was boring.

Sighing, she scored through the last line of melodramatic poetry she'd scrawled on the notepad. The only thing she liked about this new one so far was the title: *Forgotten*. She slapped the pad shut, irritated at her inability to articulate her thoughts properly.

She knew she should probably check on Zack's bodyguard. Making sure the vampire didn't go off the rails was sort of her job. Though she wasn't specifically assigned to watch over Bridget, she reasoned that working so close to them both, it would be remiss of her not to keep an eye on the undead bitch. After what had happened, she was glad she'd been overstepping her mark a little. Putting the pen down, she picked up her keys and headed reluctantly out.

Another light had gone out, this time right above her shop entrance. The arcade was pretty run down, but she couldn't afford to move to a nicer unit out on the high street, let alone the actual shopping centre along the road. The arcade sat on the outskirts of the main shopping location in town and that kept rents low. One of three security guards opened and shut the place every day and patrolled about while it was open. Larry was the only one who took the job halfway seriously, and he was also the only full-time guard, which was probably just as well.

She checked out the shop fronts as she shuffled along the corridor. Nothing much had changed since that morning. She yawned as she passed the comic book store, dawdling outside one of the two cheap fashion shops. Amira was working; the young girl had coffee-coloured skin that seemed to radiate with good health and a bright smile she pulled on only when there was some sign of rescue from her mind-numbingly dull part-time job. She lit up as her dark eyes landed on Chloe.

Chloe smiled, heading into the shop as the slender teenager opened her mouth and started chattering from her position behind the cash desk.

"Chloe, I'm *sooo* glad to see you! I'm going to be stuck here all day. I can't believe it. It's so depressing."

"All day?"

The girl pulled a face. "Dad went off to meet with another supplier or something. It all sounded very boring, and somehow I got stuck here while Ahmed gets to bugger off down to some fashion show in London."

"A fashion show?" She could barely picture Amira's loutish older brother at something so civilised.

"He wants to get off with a model. He told Dad he'd check out new suppliers." She shook her head. "I'm sure Dad knew he was lying." She leaned over the counter, folding her arms and resting on her forearms. "Anyway, what are you doing out and about?"

"I was just going to check in with Bridget," she said, shrugging slightly as she said it. "It's been a quiet morning."

"Any progress with Zack's condition?" Amira's question was hesitant but curious.

Chloe sighed inwardly. "No. Nothing."

"Sorry," she said, sounding painfully sympathetic.

"Its fine," Chloe said, knowing full-well she made it sound anything but fine. She couldn't seem to help it. Talking about it was still too hard.

"I'm sure—"

"So how are things going with that guy from school?" Chloe cut in before Amira could start a pity party for her.

She listened to her friend chat animatedly about the hot guy from her business class and wondered how much longer she could go on pretending she was okay with her own love life. It was a redundant question, and she knew it. There was nothing she could do to turn back the clock. So, she listened and she asked questions and she nodded and gasped in the right places, barely even able to keep the girl's words straight in her head as she gushed on about how amazingly smart and handsome her latest crush was. She glanced out the window when Amira's dreamy stare seemed to be going right through her. She couldn't imagine being so wrapped up in someone like that ever again, even if she did let go of her past.

She left Amira daydreaming about her crush as she headed across to Zack's agency, her eyes drifting over the name plate on the door—Z. Harrison, Private Detective. It sounded so unremarkable. He didn't advertise the psychic side of things, but word got around after he'd consulted on some cases for Shady Pines P.D. She ran her fingers over the lettering, knowing she was stalling. The chance that Zack might come out of his office while she was there made her hands shake. She'd been avoiding him as much as she could, but now she couldn't risk staying too far away.

Taking a shaky breath, she pushed the door inwards and locked eyes with the blonde vampire sitting behind the reception desk.

"Chloe," Bridget said slowly, raising a finely shaped eyebrow as the necromancer closed the door behind her.

"How's the thirst?" Chloe asked. She couldn't help but glance at Zack's closed office door briefly as she moved towards Bridget's desk.

"I'm quite full, but thanks for the offer," Bridget murmured, smiling tightly at her.

"You don't look good," she said, knowing from the look of her eyes that she was close to the edge.

Bridget's eyes looked black, her pupils enlarged. She shuddered as Chloe stopped in front of the desk. Her nostrils flared and she straightened in her seat, her energy suddenly high.

"I'm fine," she snapped.

"Yeah, that's really convincing," Chloe muttered, holding her gaze. "You're not hungry. You hear me? You've eaten today, and you're not hungry anymore."

She'd taken more than enough from Larry the night before to last her a week. Chloe knew more than she cared to about these things from her compulsory training when she 'came of age' to use her magic. She also knew that feeding directly from humans was a highly addictive thing for a vampire to do. They would crave it constantly no matter how much they drank. Bridget didn't need more blood, but she wanted it anyway. It was going to be Chloe's job to make sure she didn't get another chance at a living, breathing snack.

"Repeat after me, 'I am not hungry'."

Bridget's jaw slackened. She spoke with a frown on her pretty face. "I am not hungry."

"Good." Chloe nodded as she broke eye contact.

Bridget scowled at her as she moved away. "That is not funny."

"It wasn't supposed to be. This isn't a joke. You touch Larry again, or anyone else for that matter, and I'll report it."

She was fairly sure no one really wanted a vampire in their town, least of all the Council of necromancers. They'd tolerated her to keep Zack safe, but if she was stepping out of line, it wouldn't take much to have them turn on her.

Bridget snorted. "Larry was just convenient. You didn't seem to mind at the time or was that just to save your own precious skin?"

Chloe shuddered at the thought of letting a vampire bite her. She frowned at Bridget. "I mean it. You bite anyone else, and the necromancer's Council will be down on you like a ton of bricks."

Bridget shrugged, slender fingers going to her keyboard. "I'm not doing anything wrong."

Chloe shook her head as she left. The vampire would never listen to her threats, not really, but that didn't matter because she'd already pre-programmed her so she couldn't hurt Zack. As a necromancer, she could control Bridget, but the vampire seemed arrogant enough to assume that meant nothing more than forcing her to follow orders when she was right there in front of her. She didn't realise or remember the promise Chloe had forced from her that day. It was the only way Chloe could let her continue to watch over her ex.

She'd never trust the vampire, but she trusted her own power, and that was enough.

***

Bridget watched the punky necromancer leave, wondering what Zack had ever seen in the girl. Her lips curled as she realised whatever it had been, he certainly didn't see it anymore. She'd watched him every time they'd walked past her, and he'd never even looked twice. He didn't remember her, and he certainly wasn't drawn to her. It was slowly driving the girl crazy, and that was enough to let Bridget shrug off her warnings. Plan B was going to be more fun than she'd initially thought. Her smile widened.

Timing was going to be the key to the plan. She hummed as she brought up her copy of the details. Deleting the file wasn't necessary, it being password-protected, so she didn't need to worry about Zack reading it and it wasn't as if he was ever alone with her computer, besides. She just needed to choose a moment when the man was at his most vulnerable to disclose the details of his need for her protection. Chloe wasn't a part of those details, and even if she were she'd be a risk Bridget couldn't take. As amusing as it was to watch him fail to notice the heartbroken necromancer, there was no way she could risk sparking his curiosity. Chloe was looking too closely for an opening. Bridget could see that in the way the girl refused to keep her distance. She was going to grab hold of the first chance she got to remind Zack what she used to mean to him. That meant she was playing with fire, and she was damn well going to get burned. Bridget would make sure of that.

She picked up the phone and dialled the number of the least irritating of the necromancers residing in Shady Pines.

Kenny picked up in three rings, sounding sultry. "Hello?"

"Hey, Ken, how's the day job?"

It was a running joke between them. He slept half the day away to spend his nights watching out for threats to Zack. The hours meant he hardly ever left the apartment building he lived in, his place next door to Zack's.

"Ha ha," he muttered, yawning into her ear a second later. "Did you need something or is this a social call?"

His tone lightened at the latter suggestion.

She smiled at the thought, but she knew they couldn't let themselves get distracted. Not again. "I'll be taking babysitting duties tonight so you can get a longer lie."

"You'll be… what's happening? Has a threat been detected?"

"Nothing like that. Zack took on a case in town. We'll be looking into it later, so he'll be home late. I'll call you when he's going to get home."

"Oh. Right, cool."

He sounded suspicious, though.

Bridget pressed her lips together. The man was too smart for his own good. "I don't think we'll be really late, but I'll let you know."

"Okay, great." He paused, and for a moment, she was sure he was going to call her out on the lie. "Can you stop by after? Ten minutes or something just even."

He had that subtle hint of desperation that usually made it hard to deny him whatever he was asking.

She pulled her lower lip between her teeth. It wasn't the time to be out having careless fun. Zack's flat sat right next to Ken's. It had bad idea written all over it. She shook her head as she released her lip.

"I can't." She grimaced as she said it. Plan B was already leaving a bad taste in her mouth.

"Sure, you can," he said, sounding all husky and naked and persuasive.

She blinked. "Sure, I can."

"Great," he said, hanging up without a goodbye.

Bridget put the phone down, cursing under her breath. Necromancers! He wanted something, and she wouldn't be able to get away without giving him whatever it was. Not that he'd ever used his powers on her for that, but just knowing that he could got her all hot and shaky. His incredible physique didn't do anything to cool her down, either. No man had any right to look so damned perfect. Or smell so damned tasty…

"Shit," she hissed, feeling her fangs lengthen.

Just thinking about how he smelled was pulling her

hunger pangs back into sharp focus. She bit at her bottom lip until it bled, just to have the taste of blood fresh on her tongue. Sweet copper filled her mouth, but it wasn't enough. She *needed* more.

The jangle of Larry's keys, the echoing fall of his footsteps, snapped her attention to the hall. She knew she had to get out before she broke. One more mistake and Chloe would feed her to the dogs. She got up and darted out, focusing on making it to the fridge in her flat.

CHAPTER EIGHT

The car park didn't look menacing in the slightest, but Zack couldn't help the backward glances every time he took another step closer to the place where the girl had fallen down dead. Every step filled him with dread, the dark night air wrapping around him to stifle his breathing. This had been a bad idea. Why hadn't he known that?

He glanced at Bridget. The frosty blonde was gazing angrily into space as she walked, arms folded tightly. She didn't even look at him as he swallowed and took the last few shaky steps towards the spot he'd been standing in during the first vision. Removing one of his gloves, he crouched on the ground and placed his hand on the concrete.

The world spun as it tilted and changed around him. The girl was rushing towards her car, keys and purse in one hand. She glanced back, eyes wide in terror. Blood glimmered around her neck. She'd already been attacked. She touched her neck, and he saw the identical puncture marks as she sobbed and moved her hand back. She fell to the ground seconds later, staring lifelessly across the parking lot.

Zack glanced around, but her attacker was too far away. The vision would break if he tried to go after the guy. He'd be pulling focus away from the girl. She was the important thing here.

He looked her over. She wasn't breathing, her eyes blank. His gaze kept pulling to the wounds on her neck. A few seconds went by before he noticed Bridget was kneeling down next to him. He looked at her and the vision faded. The girl had become a ghostly whisper when he glanced back down again. She blinked out of existence quickly.

"He must have stabbed her in the neck," he said softly.

"What did you see?" Bridget straightened herself back to a standing position.

"She was running. She fell. Her neck was… it looked like a vampire bite."

He laughed at what he'd just said. It sounded just as ridiculous out loud as he'd thought it had in his head.

"Well," Bridget said. "That's not good. Did you see the vampire?"

"Vampires aren't a real thing."

Why wasn't she scoffing at what he'd said? Surely, she couldn't possibly…

"We need to talk," she told him.

"Uh, what do you mean?" He was just being paranoid.

She looked deadly serious. "There's something you need to know about your condition."

"My condition?" Did she mean the amnesia or the weird mental breaks he usually had after a vision? Both would fit the bill.

"You're never going to get your memory back," she told him. "There's a reason for that. We should talk, in private."

"What do you mean, I'm never getting it back?"

Panic flared at the very thought of it. He felt his chest tighten, and he had to remind himself to suck in a breath. He didn't think amnesia was such a categorical, definitive thing, so how could she say that? The doctors themselves had told him they couldn't say for sure if he'd regain his memories or not. Bridget was just a cop; she hardly qualified as a medical professional. He narrowed his eyes. "You can't know that. Not for sure."

She sighed. "Let's just go to your place, Zack. I'll explain everything when we get inside."

He had half a mind to tell her to get lost. "I didn't have an episode. Right after the vision."

She shrugged. "It was the second time you went into it."

"Aye, maybe that's it," he muttered, not quite sure what to think. It was the first time he'd felt stable after a vision. Maybe he was getting better. He could only hope.

Bridget's words burrowed deeper into his worry as they walked. He'd been so sure his memories would come back, someway, somehow. Never was a fucking long time to be stumbling around not sure of who he was, where he'd come from. He didn't know how he'd cope with that if it were true. He didn't even know what had happened to trigger the amnesia. How the hell could Bridget know he wouldn't get his memory back? Did that mean she knew what had happened that night? What had she been holding back from him? She'd had his blind trust, but did she really deserve it?

They walked towards his block of flats. He felt weird about having her back at his place. Their relationship had always been strictly professional. This seemed too intimate. He couldn't even remember the last time he'd had a girl in his flat. He snorted at that stupid joke as he let her into the building. For all he knew, he'd been great with the ladies. Somehow, he doubted it.

"So this is it," he said, unlocking the door and motioning to her to go inside.

The door opened across from them. He smiled tightly at the second cop assigned to supposedly 'protect' him.

The guy looked Bridget over and smiled broadly. "How's it going?"

She ignored him and went inside. Zack caught the derision on her face and hid a smile of his own. Kenny was a sleaze. He'd known that before he made the mistake of touching stuff in his flat. Everything in the place was swamped in a haze of carnal desire. The guy had sex on the brain twenty-four-seven. Zack was never setting foot in the place ever again.

He didn't bother greeting the cop. He just followed Bridget into his own flat and closed the door. She'd found the living room by the time he'd locked the door behind him.

"Very understated," she said, motioning to the room as she sat down on the sofa.

He shrugged, wanting her to get to the damn point. He was irritable enough already.

"So, what was it you had to tell me in private?"

Her lips twitched into a small smile briefly before she spoke. "This is going to sound crazy when I start, but stick with me. It gets good."

"I'm all ears," he said, sitting on the armchair. It was lovingly handcrafted using material hand-woven with care, so he took his gloves off and basked in the sense of contentment soaked into the chair as his bare fingers touched the fabric.

"There's a reason I was sent here to protect you."

He knew that. He'd been given a lot of vague hints about the reason for it as he was being discharged from the hospital under Bridget's watchful eyes. He'd almost died because he knew something. Something he couldn't remember now, no matter how hard he tried. The doctors had said the dissociative episodes he was having were his brain trying to keep him from uncovering that information. It was something he couldn't handle knowing. His mind was protecting itself.

"Vampires are real, Zack."

The deadpan delivery and the absurdity of her words tickled something in him that made him burst into such peals of laughter that he could barely breathe through. When he was wiping the tears from the corners of his eyes, he managed to bark out, "Shut up."

"They did this to you," she told him, not even cracking a smile. She looked deadly serious in spite of his hysterics. "They're the reason I was sent here to protect you."

A stab of terror hit him and he pushed it back. It wasn't true. She was a liar. *Very funny, Bridget. Get to the punch-line already.*

"This is a wind up. Don't be such a bitch," he snapped, taking his hands from the arm rests of the wonderful chair. "It isn't funny."

"It's not supposed to be funny." She opened her mouth as if to grin.

Her teeth sharpened suddenly, her pupils dilating rapidly at the same time.

What the hell? He stared as she bit her own hand with those crazy-sharp teeth. He wanted to get up and run in the face of such crazy behaviour, but his body felt frozen in place. What he'd just seen wasn't real. It couldn't be. This was completely fucked up. He blinked.

His memory flashed back to the drink he'd spilled on the floor of the office. The red stuff that had looked suspiciously like…"Holy shit!"

She licked at her lips as she withdrew her teeth from her hand and shoved it in front of him. "Is this what that girl's wound looked like?"

He nodded slowly. The wound was virtually identical to what he'd seen. How…? He frowned.

She rolled her eyes. Her teeth were back to normal when she spoke, but her mouth looked red.

"It wasn't me. When exactly do you think I'd have time for that?" She screwed up her nose. "Besides, I don't bite humans."

"But you do drink blood. That's what's always in your cup."

He couldn't believe he'd said that out loud…and that she was humouring him enough to not laugh in his face.

She nodded, her gaze level. "You're handling this remarkably well."

"It only looks like it. I'm freaking out on the inside," he said, wondering when he'd black out.

This type of information should have been enough to make his protective brain go into overdrive. Maybe it wasn't happening because he didn't really believe it. It hadn't sunk in yet.

"It's bad news that there's another vampire in town," she said, bringing her wounded hand to her mouth and sucking on it.

It was weirdly sexy if he didn't think about what she was actually doing right now—sucking the blood from her hand. She stopped and gazed at him thoughtfully.

He noticed her hand was healing when she dropped it back to her lap.

"But there's no need to worry. I won't allow that vampire to touch you," she told him. "You won't be harmed. Not while I'm around."

"Okay," he said, blinking, not sure what else to say. He appreciated her devotion to his safety, but right now, he was still trying to grasp the idea that vampires were real. He couldn't quite reconcile the concept with his basic common sense; it just didn't want to compute. "What's it like being a vampire?"

"It's fun, but it has a downside. Like everything, I suppose." She smiled as if it wasn't life changing information she was talking here.

"Are you staying here tonight?"

He wasn't sure why he'd asked. He supposed he didn't like the thought of being bitten while he slept, and she'd been protecting him for six months now. If he couldn't trust her, who could he trust?

"Do you need me to do that, Zack?"

He flushed. "No. I just wasn't sure what it meant that there was another vampire around. Will he try to attack me?"

"Kenny's right next door. He won't let you come to harm."

"Right. But the vampire will try to attack me?"

She nodded slowly. "It's likely that he'll try to bring you to his clan. The clans value humans who have psychic abilities. They make even more valuable vampires. That's why you've been targeted, Zack."

He stared at her, horror filling him. Could this get any worse? "What are you saying?"

"I'm saying they want to make you one of them."

She paused just long enough for him to know she wasn't sure about going on. When she opened her mouth again, he knew by the look in her eyes that what she said next was going to be awful. Dread built up like solidifying cement in his gut.

"Forget every vampire movie you've ever seen. Turning into a vampire isn't the cakewalk they make it out to be. You don't just get sucked on and then drink the blood of your Master and wake up changed. It's a major ritual that can last for days. There's usually a blood orgy going on by the end. Your Master has to kill you in an extremely violent, painful way. With regular vampires, it's brutal enough. Psychic humans being turned are on another level. Whatever skill you have determines what your maker does to torture you before he kills you. It's supposed to make your abilities stronger, but it's a superstitious practice. You have visions, so he'd most likely gouge out your eyes. They'd grow back, but they wouldn't be quite the same. They'd be all… demonic-looking. You'd never be mistaken for human again. Anyway…" She shrugged as if it wasn't a big deal before opening her mouth to tell him more awful things, no doubt.

No fucking way. He couldn't let her go on. "Stop. Stop right there."

This was worse than he could have imagined. He didn't want to know anything else. At least, not about what the vampires were likely to do to him. "Wait. How did you become a vampire?"

She frowned, pursing her lips. Shaking her head, she folded her arms. "I don't remember now. Undoubtedly, it was brutal and disgusting. Those are our ways. We don't turn people who won't know and agree to those conditions up front. If you're squeamish, this isn't the life for you."

"I would never agree to that shit," he said, relief spilling into his voice.

"The exception would be your kind," she said, smiling ruefully. "Your skills are so sought after, they wouldn't care that they were turning you by force. It's supposed to enhance any psychic ability tenfold to turn a human with abilities by force. I don't believe that, it's superstitious nonsense, but the older vampires swear by it, and they're the ones who sign off on all that ritualistic stuff."

"Fuck," he swore, tugging at his hair. He couldn't take this in. It was just too much, and much too horrifying. His thoughts were spinning. "I seriously doubt I'm going to be able to sleep tonight. You do realise that?"

"Well, I have to go." She got up.

He stared at her incredulously. Dropping a bomb like that and running away; she had to be taking the piss.

"Wait. Can you not just stay?"

She shook her head. "I have to get dinner."

He almost offered to cook before he realised what she meant. His thoughts went back to her 'diet mix', and his heart sank. "You don't eat normal food at all, do you?"

She grinned. Her teeth were still slightly bloody from sucking on her hand. He shuddered.

"Do I look like I eat solid food?" She did a quick twirl that emphasised her model-like figure and ballet dancer's grace.

"No, I suppose not." Her effort to lighten the mood fell short. He tried to smile, but it came out more like a grimace.

"Don't worry, Zack. I don't feed on humans." She stroked the side of his face gently. Her fingers were cold, making him shiver. "I'll see you at work."

"What about—"

"Don't worry about the vampire. I'll deal with him tonight."

She left, and he quickly locked the door behind her. Everything felt out of whack. His thoughts were all over the place, his breathing was quickening, and he was heading into a full tilt panic if he wasn't careful. He seriously needed to calm the fuck down.

He went to the fridge, stared inside, and shut the door again. Eating was out. His stomach was churning, anyway. He doubted he'd enjoy a single bite. He'd be lucky if he could keep anything down. Sleeping wasn't an option, either. Not with his everything that was going through his head.

He paced around, picking up his phone and putting it back down again several times in a row. Wanting to call his sister, he resisted. She always called him. She'd call. He just had to wait.

***

Bridget walked into Kenny's apartment and closed the door quietly behind her. He had his lips pressed to hers within seconds, his arms on either side of her as he pushed her up against the door. She stroked his naked back as she opened her mouth to his probing tongue. He pulled back quickly, licking at his lips and scowling.

"You taste like blood. Did that freak let you drink from him?"

She grinned. It wasn't often that she saw the jealous side of her secret lover. "So what if he did?"

Anger sparked in his eyes. "I don't want you putting your mouth anywhere near that—"

"Relax," she told him. "I bit my hand. I was given instructions to educate him about vampires, and he didn't believe what I was telling him. He just needed to see it for himself."

He frowned. "Bet that made him spaz out. I'm not going

to have to deal with another breakdown, am I?"

"I don't think so," she said, wrapping her arms around his neck. He felt so good pressed against her, half-dressed like this. She fought back a blissful sigh. He didn't need the ego boost. "He took it well. I think he might be stabilizing."

"Well, good. That means more time for us," he said, kissing her again.

He never really cared if she tasted like blood. Who she'd gotten it from was a different story; if he knew about Larry, he'd pitch a fit and go beat the poor kid up over it. But the taste never bothered him. It was rare for a human not to get squeamish, but a necromancer? Most of them would rather stick their tongues into an electrical socket than kiss a vampire. There was something so intoxicating about his unconditional desire for her.

As much as she wanted to indulge him, she had a vampire to hunt down and take care of. Without knowing which clan was invading town, she'd have her work cut out for her.

Just five minutes, she told herself.

She was lying to herself, and she knew it. It was never just five minutes. Not with Kenny. Five minutes and she wouldn't care. Five minutes and nothing would tear her away from him. A hundred vampires could descend on Zack's flat to rip him to shreds. She still wouldn't be able to tell Kenny to get off her. She wouldn't want to.

"I have to go," she murmured as he started unbuttoning her shirt.

"You need to stay," he said, not looking up. "It's been too long."

"We have jobs to do."

"I don't care."

She saw the all-consuming desire in his eyes when he looked back at her.

"You're taking too long," she complained. "Rip the damn shirt."

She pulled at his jeans, and the fly fell open. He wasn't wearing underwear. As usual, she felt overdressed compared to him.

Her shirt ripped open, and she gasped. No matter how many times he did that, she always got a little thrill from it. This time, her thrill was mixing uncontrollably with the flash of hunger always just there under the surface now that she'd tasted human blood again. Kenny's throbbing veins were driving her crazy with blood-lust. Her fangs shot into place.

He looked at her face and smiled slyly. "You want my blood."

She couldn't deny it. Her body craved everything he had.

"Taste me," he whispered.

He shuffled slightly, and his jeans fell to the floor. She fought to contain her hunger as he stepped out of them and positioned his throat in front of her. His hands opened her trousers and one slipped inside her pants while the other unclasped her bra.

"You really want this?"

"I've wanted it since the second I laid eyes on you."

She moaned as his fingers worked their magic. He always knew exactly how to touch her. She positioned her fangs over his vein and bit into this skin. He gasped. The pain of her teeth sinking into his flesh would be gone within seconds, replaced by a euphoric high she gifted him through her saliva. Her own high was doubled up by his well-positioned fingers as his warm blood filled her eager mouth.

***

Chloe tapped her pen on the counter as she waited for the kettle to boil. Her notepad sat open in front of her, the blank page taunting her. She wasn't sure when exactly the writer's block had crept in, but it had been after she'd lost Zack. It still felt weird to see him around, knowing what they'd had and that he didn't remember a second of their time together. She mourned the loss of him as if he'd died that night. He'd been taken from her as finally as if he had.

The town had been infested, and the Council of necromancers had been stretched thin dealing with the problem. Zack had been home, in the town over, Riverton. His family had bought the closest house to the edge of town, a recluse's mansion built in the woods, and they had been living there for years when the worst had finally happened. They'd known about vampires; they'd known about necromancers. They'd known they were at risk of being targeted if anyone found out what they could do, but they'd also known Shady Pines was full of necromancers. They'd thought they were close enough to town to be covered by that protection. It turned out they'd been wrong.

She sighed. The two of them had talked about getting a place together, in town. She'd spent so long cursing their indecision after what happened. It had been all she could think about for so damned long.

If only. Those two little words had a strangle-hold on her heart. She hadn't even found out what had happened until the next morning, after she'd texted Zack. He'd never sent her a message back, and she'd decided to go to his house. By the time she'd been dressed and picking up her jacket to leave, the phone had been ringing. She'd answered it, being told what had happened by one of the Council Elders and warned not to approach him. She'd ignored the idiotic warning and rushed to the hospital to see him, but she'd known the moment he looked at her that he had no idea who she was. She'd feigned confusion and apologised that she'd gotten the wrong room as she'd left. Thinking about it hurt like hell.

The briefing from the Council had taken an hour or so, and most of it had sounded like white noise at the time. She'd been warned off being around him, of giving him any reminders of their 'old' life together. Not that she even wanted to go through the pain of having to tell him what they'd meant to each other. He should just *know*. He should be able to look at her and know beyond a shadow of a doubt that she meant something to him. It stung that he didn't.

Sighing, she put the pen down and fixed herself a cup of tea. It was useless going over it all. There was nothing she could do.

She'd seen it a million times in silly soap operas; the wife or husband of the amnesiac breaking their hearts trying to convince their other half that they belonged together. It wasn't worth going through that. He'd never fall for her the same way he had the first time around. They'd been pushed together by circumstances beyond their control. It had been more than a girl falling for a guy she thought was cute or a guy asking out a girl because he couldn't stop thinking about her. It had been so far beyond the superficial that she had always believed it had been arranged by fate.

She sipped at her tea and wondered what it meant when fate unmade its decisions. Was she really ever supposed to fall for a painfully shy neurotic with the strangest psychic ability she'd ever heard of? Had he ever really been meant to see past her defences to the true romantic inside?

She supposed time would tell. She put down her empty mug with a sigh.

Maybe it already had.

***

It was vaguely disturbing how many cracks there were in his ceiling. Zack gave up counting them and tried to figure out the weird circular mark in the middle. He assumed the light fitting used to be there rather than directly over the bed. He pulled at his gloves.

Wishing Bridget had stayed to watch over him, he supposed the only good thing was she wouldn't realise exactly how weird he was. The gloves hadn't always been a night-time feature, but considering emotional resonances seemed to be harder to shrug off when he was unconscious, he didn't like to take chances when he slept. His naked chest enjoyed the warmth of the covers without any ill feeling. His hands wouldn't be quite so easily satisfied.

He lay awake thinking of Bridget's scarily sharp teeth. The woman was beautiful, and those teeth hadn't changed that; they'd only shown him that she was also deadly.

Vampires were real.

He didn't relish the idea, particularly considering he was a desired possession to their kind. Shivering, he pulled the duvet closer. He couldn't shake the horrifying mental image she'd given him when she'd told him so casually that the vampires would most likely gouge his eyes out.

He really wished Audrey would call. He could use the reassurance that Bridget was crazy or that he was. Vampires couldn't be real. That was insane.

"What's the matter, Zack?"

Audrey's voice made him smile.

"Thank God," he said. "Where have you been? I need to talk to you."

"I've been a little busy."

"Too busy to call your little brother?"

She just laughed.

He sighed. "I've been told something about what happened to me. I'm kind of freaked out by it."

"Oh? Who told you what?"

"Bridget. She told me—" he cut himself off, feeling like a moron.

"Bridget?" Audrey sounded lost. "Doesn't sound familiar. Who the hell is Bridget?"

"What do you mean, who the hell is Bridget?" He couldn't believe she didn't know. "What are you, high?"

"Ah, she's that woman from the FBU," she said. "What did she tell you?"

"Vampires," he spat out, cringing as he waited for her reply.

"She told you what happened?"

He stared at the ceiling. "So it's true?"

"That depends on what she told you."

"Vampires are after me."

Audrey sighed. "That sounds about right."

"Shit," he swore softly.

"They won't get you," she said. "Shady Pines is full of necromancers."

He blinked, wondering if she'd really just said what he thought she had. "It's full of what?"

"People who can control the dead."

"Okay, I'm hanging up now. This isn't funny anymore." She was messing with him; she had to be.

She laughed. "You get visions and read emotional imprints from inanimate objects. Is it really so hard to believe in vampires and necromancers?"

"Aye, it is," he said, feeling defensive.

"Well, then. You need to wake up, little Z. The world is darker than you know."

He frowned. "What's that supposed to mean?"

"It means you need to watch your back. Don't trust this Bridget woman, whoever she is."

"But I—" He cut himself off when he realised Audrey was gone.

His elusive sister had hung up on him. He sighed as he closed his eyes and attempted to get to sleep.

***

Bridget left Kenny's house wearing one of his sweaters over her torn shirt. It was close to midnight, and she hadn't bothered trying to talk him into letting her leave. She'd just waited until he'd fallen asleep. Her torn shirt wasn't anywhere close to decent, so she'd thrown on a sweater she knew he'd worn recently. It contained his scent, and she was going to go home and sleep in it. He might not get it back at all.

The night sky was clear, the stars shining brightly overhead. It wasn't her job to track vampires, but she thought about hunting down the one who'd bitten that girl. He was a threat to Zack. Taking care of threats to Zack's safety definitely fell within her job description.

She called Rick as she walked. As usual, he wasn't closely monitoring his calls. She eventually got his voicemail and decided not to bother leaving a message. She rolled her eyes and put the phone away.

She went home and scooped up one of her precious cats. Arthur hissed as she bit into her hand and pressed the wound to his brother's mouth. The twitching of Lancelot's whiskers was followed by the lapping of his little tongue. Arthur hissed again. It wasn't favouritism that directed her choice tonight. Lancelot was faster on his feet, but Arthur was just an animal. Jealousy was instinctive.

She opened the front door and placed Lancelot outside. He sat on the doormat for a moment, cleaning his paws. Bridget picked up Arthur as he dug his claws into her legs.

He wriggled in her arms, not as content as usual. She presented him the wound she'd opened after a moment's hesitation. He purred as he drank a few drops of her blood. When she put him down, he shot out of the front door, making Lancelot's hair stand on end.

"There's a good boy," she said with a smile and raised eyebrows.

Favouritism apparently counted for something, after all. Lancelot meowed at her as she closed the door on him. He sat on the welcome mat, licking his paw. His sister and brother were fast asleep under the radiator in the living room. She left them be and went into her bedroom to concentrate.

She lay down and reached out with her thoughts to Arthur. The link between familiar and vampire was strong and grew stronger every time she utilised it. She saw through his eyes as he ran through an alley. She didn't bother attempting to figure out where he was. He knew he was out there to track down the other vampire. He wouldn't stop until he'd found him. She'd be sure to look for clues when he did. She heard him hiss and realised Lancelot had followed him only when she saw the other cat through Arthur's eyes. The strange point of view made Lancelot look weak and pathetic. Arthur's hissing was followed by a swat of his paw, claws out. Lancelot mewled sadly. He darted out of Arthur's way as her favourite pet continued forward.

The night didn't seem quite so dark anymore. The streetlights illuminated Arthur's path. He stopped suddenly, and Bridget saw the vampire standing in front of the arcade.

It was definitely a man, and not an unattractive one at that. He had something in his hand. The door swung inwards, and he went inside. Arthur rushed forward, but the door closed before he could follow him inside. He leapt at the door, his paws reaching for the handle.

Bridget sat up, opened her eyes, and broke the visual link with her redirection of focus. She stalked out of the house, only slowing down to pick up a golf umbrella from the rack at the building's entry on her way out.

The arcade was dark, lights out for the night. The sign above the doorway was lit up, making her smile wryly. Something had been wrong with the bulbs in the middle word ever since she'd been there, turning 'Shady Pines Arcade' into simply 'Shady Arcade'. It had never been fixed and never would be. Six months in town and it was one thing she knew for sure.

She opened the door; Arthur awaited her instructions. She stroked his fluffy head and told him to go home. She didn't speak the words aloud, just used their telepathic link to show him the front door of the flat.

He sauntered off when she straightened up. She went into the arcade, clutching the umbrella around the middle as she walked. Her heels clicked on the tiled floor. The vampire would know someone was following him. She wondered if she'd get to find out who he was before she killed him.

"Stop right where you are." His nasal voice penetrated the darkness.

She sensed him straight ahead. It was too dark to make

out more than a vague shape where he stood. He was big and tall, but he smelled new. Younger vampires tended to smell less dead. Anything over a century old had a rotting carcass scent that made Bridget gag when she got within a few feet of them. This guy was freshly made. She grinned into the darkness.

"You're in my town," she told him.

"This is necromancer territory," he said, sounding cocky. "What the hell's a vampire doing messing about here?"

"Funny," she said. "I was about to ask you the same thing."

"I know who you are," he said. "You don't scare me."

"Well, I don't know who you are, and you don't scare me either."

He took a few steps closer and she was able to see his face. It wasn't good enough. She needed to see more skin. A positive ID was more important than dispatching him. She had to know which clan was after Zack. Whichever one knew about him, they certainly wouldn't tell any of the others. She would earn her bosses' eternal trust if she could just disarm this newly hatched vampire.

"You look better than the last one they sent."

He frowned at her. "I would do. I'm the first."

She laughed, making sure to make the sound deep and throaty. It was her sexiest laugh. Kenny couldn't listen to it without stretching out the front of his jeans. "You really believe that?"

His glare was searing as he approached. She dropped the umbrella. Staking him was out of the question. She wondered if this would be what landed her a promotion. Not that it mattered.

She reached out and touched his arm, thinking of Kenny and the new development in their sexual relationship. She bit at her lip, drawing blood.

The new vampire was young enough to be teased by the scent of it. His expression went from guarded to slack and ravenous within seconds.

"I haven't been around another vampire in ages," she said with a soft sigh. "I haven't gotten laid in a long time."

His eyes, already desirous at the sight of the blood on her lip, turned almost feral. She smiled. Her plan might have been hackneyed and obvious, but he was falling for it all the same.

She hauled off Kenny's sweater. Her ripped shirt hung open, allowing him a glimpse of her lacy bra.

The vampire made to grab her and she took a step back, shaking her head.

"I took *my* top off," she said, fingers tugging at the hem of his turtleneck.

It took the dimwit a second to realise what she was alluding to. He hauled his top off a second later. Her fingers trailed down his hard, muscled chest. His skin was unmarked.

He pulled her to him and pressed his mouth to hers, first sucking at the blood on her lower lip and then plunging his tongue into her mouth. She fought the urge to pull away, her fingers exploring his naked back. The branding wasn't there, either.

Damn it! She unbuttoned his trousers, pushing them to the ground as he grabbed at her tits. He was rock-hard against her as she went for the next most likely area. *Bingo*, she thought as she stroked the raised skin on his ass. She traced the pattern a few times to make sure she was right about it. The half-moon design with the 'W' across it was similar to another clan's design. She checked around and didn't find any little bumps that might signify stars. It was safe to assume that he was with the Winter clan.

She pushed him back. He stumbled, tripping over the trousers pooled at his ankles. She wiped her mouth and picked up the umbrella. His mouth moved, but he didn't get the chance to ask her what she was doing. She staked him through the heart with the silver-tipped, pointed end of the umbrella. His body turned into a pile of black ash, a jangling sound telling her the keys he'd used to gain entry were under the lump somewhere. She picked them out as a smile broke out on her face. She might have taken a groping from a thoroughly stupid vampire, but at least she had something good to show for it.

The keys belonged to Larry. She read his name on the keyring and shook her head as she dropped them again. The greasy security guard would get the blame for the mess and the door being left open. He would be too dead to care. The vampire had been out of control. Whether he'd turned Larry or killed him, she supposed she'd find out soon enough. She fished the vampire's clothes out of the dust pile and tossed them into the nearest bin. The pile of ash, she left spattered over the floor. For a second, she considered finding a way to clean up the mess. She knew Chloe would know what the ash really was. She'd likely inform her Council.

Bridget smiled. All she'd done was protect Zack. They couldn't penalize her for it. So she'd end up having to talk to someone about what had happened, probably Chloe. It was almost enough to make her consider breaking into the cleaner's cupboard to find the vacuum cleaner. Almost. She shrugged, kicking at the idiot's remains. She could deal with one little necromancer.

She threw her sweater back on and headed home, leaving the arcade unlocked.

CHAPTER NINE

It was early, and he was far too tired to put up with the canned coffee that tasted vaguely of depression. Zack's complete lack of sleep had made him cranky. He'd started at every little noise the house had made the night before, convinced a vampire was breaking in to poke out his eyes and laugh maniacally about it while he screamed until his sanity broke for good. He was going to start wearing sunglasses. His eyes seemed woefully under-protected.

The arcade was open and the smell of Cassandra's baking filling his nostrils as he drifted into the building. He headed towards her cafe, knowing it would be closed but wanting to get a closer smell, anyway. He usually slipped his lunch order under the door while she was closed, along with the cash to pay for it. Today, he added a breakfast order and hoped she would see it soon. Whatever muffins were on the menu, he could tell they were going to be even more amazing than usual. Getting them while they were hot would be absolute bliss.

He walked away from the cafe with a pained sigh. His

office was open as was usual with an early-to-rise bodyguard. He wondered exactly what time Bridget got there every day as he glanced at her black ceramic drink container. How could he not have noticed what she was sooner?

"Hey, Zack," she said, barely glancing up from her computer screen.

It was as if nothing had even changed. He supposed for her, not much had.

"Cassandra should be by soon. Let me know when she comes." He went into his office and closed the door.

Was it all some weird-ass dream? Had to be. Had to be.

He sat behind his desk and tried to relax. Everything was completely normal. He hadn't seen fang marks on a murdered girl's throat. He hadn't seen Bridget grow fangs and bite her own hand.

He got up and went back into the reception area, looking Bridget over. She was too pretty to be human. Her icy-blue eyes locked on him as he took in the pale perfection of her skin. She wasn't breathing. He realised it after a few minutes of regarding her in complete silence. He hadn't dreamt what she'd shown him. He wasn't crazy. She really was a vampire. He swallowed as he met her eyes.

"Am… am I safe?"

She raised an eyebrow, briefly. "I told you I would take care of it, and I have."

He frowned. "What does that mean?"

"It means you don't need to worry about any blood-sucking fiends."

"What about the girl?"

"What about her?"

"Is she dead, or…" He didn't want to have to say it.

The door opened, and Cassandra entered with a bag and a cup in her hands. She looked as radiant as ever, her caramel skin flawless and her deep brown eyes bright. The top she wore had been a gift from one of the other shop owners in the arcade. It had that cheap and tacky look to it. He appreciated the low cut front as much as any guy would, but it was pretty revealing for her to be wearing out in public, at least during the day. He doubted it was something she'd put on if it hadn't been given to her. She was too nice for her own good.

He smiled as he took his order out of her hands, wishing he'd thought to take his gloves off when she appeared. He was sure he wouldn't get any nasty surprises from touching her.

"Thanks. Smells amazing."

"Aw, you're too sweet," she told him, rubbing his arm before she took off. "See you at lunch time."

She never made a big deal out of his constant use of the gloves. It was like she didn't even notice he was a freak.

"Don't even think about asking her out," Bridget snapped, looking as if she wanted to break the pen she held in half.

"I wasn't."

He knew his face was going red, but he would never admit he fancied Cassandra. Everyone had to fancy her. She was a goddess.

He retreated into his office and started in on his

breakfast. His stomach told him he was full after one muffin, but he couldn't let the other one go to waste. He carefully collected every moreish crumb in his naked fingers and demolished every last bite before he put the empty bag into the waste basket. The coffee lasted slightly longer, but only because it was a large cup.

The creak of his door made him glance up quickly.

Bridget gave him a rueful smile. "We have a problem."

She opened the door wider, and the boy with the pink purse, Dorian, entered. His eyes were big, and Zack could tell from where he sat that he was shaking uncontrollably.

Bridget ushered him into the room and closed the door behind the three of them.

"What's wrong?"

Zack loathed to ask because he knew the answer wasn't going to be pleasant.

"Tell him what you told me," Bridget said in a soft quiet voice that Zack wished she would use more often. It was very soothing, and it seemed to stop the kid from shaking quite so violently.

"My sister came back," he said, swallowing audibly. "She's not right in the head."

"She bit his dad," Bridget said when Dorian appeared to be done with his story in favour of adopting a blank gaze that burned into the wall behind Zack.

Zack didn't know what to say. The girl had been turned into a vampire. He had no words to make it better. He threw Bridget a look, wondering exactly what she expected him to do. She prodded the boy in the arm. He leaned forward and dropped something onto the table in front of Zack. The garment was pink. Blood-stained. He was pretty sure it was the T-shirt the girl had been wearing when she'd dropped dead.

"Think you can check out his story?" Bridget pushed the shirt a little bit closer to him.

He fought the urge to recoil. His fingers were still naked and vulnerable. Touching the bloodied item didn't appeal to him, but he didn't think he had much of a choice. Bridget's steely blue eyes were staring him down, unblinking, challenging him to defy her.

He frowned as he picked the T-shirt up. The vision was no more than a quick flash of memory.

The girl had gone home and picked a fight with her parents, which had quickly escalated to baring her newly acquired fangs and lunging at them. Her father screamed at the bite she took out of his arm. A piece of flesh ripped from it as he grabbed his arm away from her hungry mouth. She turned away when the two of them ran into the bathroom and closed the door. They were yelling for help as she stripped off her clothes and headed down the basement stairs.

He put the T-shirt down. "Vampires are real."

He wished he hadn't touched the damned thing.

"They are?" The kid had finally found his tongue.

"Oh, they most definitely are," Bridget assured. "When she goes out, you need to have a priest bless your house. She won't be able to step past the threshold if you do that."

"She can't be… I thought… Vampires can't enter the

homes of the living?" The kid looked confused.

"There's an exception to that rule. She used to live there, so she can walk in any time she likes unless the house is protected against her kind."

The boy's eyes seemed to regain their focus as he looked curiously at Bridget. "You know a lot about this stuff."

She nodded. "Where's your sister right now?"

"Oh, uh, she went into the basement and stayed there. I mean, after she freaked Mum and Dad out. They almost called the police."

Almost? Zack glanced at Bridget.

"They rationalised what happened," Bridget said.

The kid nodded slowly. "Dad bandaged his arm, and Mum made tea. Like nothing had happened."

"Is there someone you can stay with?" Bridget was asking the kid.

"I don't… I'm supposed to be at school."

"Okay," she said. "Is there a friend's house you could go to after school?"

"I suppose…" He didn't look sure.

Zack watched Bridget, wondering what was on her mind. He got the gut-clenching feeling they were going to hunt down the vampire. He wondered where he could get a pair of sunglasses from before they went.

"Here's what's going to happen," Bridget said, taking charge in her bossy tone. "You're going to tell me your address, and you're going to go to school. You'll go to a friend's house after, and don't come home until late."

The kid frowned. He was shaking again. "Are you going

to… I mean, I know she's not my sister anymore, but she… she still looks like she is."

Bridget pursed her lips. She stared into Dorian's eyes. "You will write down your home address on this piece of paper. You will go to school and to your friend's house after that."

He gazed blankly at her, and Zack knew Bridget was compelling him somehow. The thought gave him shivers. He really needed to get himself a pair of sunglasses. He didn't even care if they were angry sunglasses.

The kid scribbled down a barely legible address before he left, walking like a robot. Zack read the address and glanced at his vampire bodyguard.

"You can't go out in sunlight."

"It's overcast outside," she told him with a smirk. "We've got a baby vampire to stake."

"But…you're a vampire. Doesn't that mean some of them are…sort of okay?"

She laughed.

"So that's what you think of me? Sort of okay?" Her eyes sparkled.

He wondered if she expected a compliment. A girl like her was probably used to being told how good she looked. "Well, you know what I mean. You're not a bad person."

"No, I'm not," she said. "The girl was created by someone who is out to get you, Zack. Chances are, she has your details. I might have killed her creator, but his weapon is still out there right now, loaded and waiting to strike."

"Oh," he said, wishing it didn't sound so horrifying.

"Don't worry. She won't get anywhere near you." She picked up the piece of paper with the address on it.

***

Chloe turned Larry's keys over in her hand. She'd been one of the first into the building when the cleaners were finishing up. Mary had handed her the keys, smiling wryly. She'd thought he had dropped them and left without locking the doors. Someone had gotten in and tried to light a fire. Mary liked him, so she'd tidied the mess and figured Chloe would be the best one to leave them with. She didn't want Larry getting in trouble with building management.

Chloe had frowned as she took in Mary's story. She'd asked what she meant by saying someone had tried to start a fire. It turned out she'd found a pile of black ash, the keys lying on the ground close to it.

Chills had run down Chloe's spine at the image the cleaner had planted in her head. Had Bridget done something to Larry? Her suspicions faded quickly as she realised the time frame didn't allow for her friend to be turned and then staked. It was probably coincidental. She shivered.

The blonde vampire had most likely compelled Larry to give her the keys. It would be too much to hope for that Bridget might be the pile of ash the cleaners had binned.

She confirmed it wasn't when she heard the bitch's heels clacking out there not long after she'd gotten to her own shop. She peered out, getting a quick look. Bridget was most definitely not the pile of ash. That meant another vampire had been in town. Not just in town, but in the arcade. She knew what that meant, and it made her stomach clench.

Picking up the phone, she called her contact on the Council. Every necromancer was assigned one when they passed their training. A senior person they could turn to, someone who would decide when the Elders were needed. She shivered again, pulling on her jacket as she dialled.

"Hello?" He cleared his throat, sounding groggy as he answered.

"Kenny, something's happened. We need the Elders."

He sighed, and she pictured him rolling his eyes. He'd never had much patience with her. She'd seen him shake his head at her decisions too many times. This was different. He had to see how important this was.

"What is it this time?"

She closed her eyes and tried to summon some patience. "There was a vampire in the arcade."

"Was?"

"He or she was staked. The point is—"

"So there's no problem."

"You're not listening." Her voice had taken on a sharp tone. She couldn't seem to help it when she spoke to her contact. She'd requested a new one several times. Apparently, someone high up hated her because she was still stuck with Kenny the Dick.

"Bridget will have gotten rid of it. Vampires aren't a problem, *Zoe*. We have complete power over them."

"But something's—" She narrowed her eyes at the phone as she removed it from her ear. The dial tone sounded insufferably loud. She slammed the receiver down hard, sending a shock of pain up her arm. "Damn it!"

She didn't know why she'd called that idiot. He only ever wound her up and made her want to punch something hard enough to shatter bone. Whatever was going on, she was going to figure out what to do on her own. If there'd been a vampire sniffing around the arcade, there was no doubt he'd been after Zack. The species didn't generally risk coming to necromancer towns. There had to be something worth coming for.

She tapped Larry's keys with her nails. One vampire wouldn't usually be a problem. It was what that one vampire's appearance signified that was the issue. One of the clans knew about Zack. They would send more.

***

Zack's insistence on stopping to buy sunglasses made Bridget tetchy. He said it would only take a minute and then he stalked down the arcade, peering into the shop windows as he passed. The shop that supplied Cassandra's work wear sold women's clothes only. He'd leave it off as a last resort, certain he'd end up with something with pink frames or rhinestones if he ventured inside. The alternative store a few shops down seemed more hopeful. He could see a stand with leather cuffs, earrings, and sunglasses that looked at least unisex.

Bridget was at his side within seconds. She put her hand on his arm. "We should go."

He couldn't put his finger on it, but there was something

in her voice that told him there was more to her protest than the risk of burning five minutes of daylight.

"I'll only be a minute," he insisted, pushing the door open and breaking her grip on his arm. He glanced at her as he went inside. Her face was rigid. She was pissed. He let the door swing shut behind him.

The girl behind the counter glanced his way and did a double take. He sighed inwardly. People were always weirded out by the reclusive amnesiac. A second later, she was smiling stiffly and busying herself with something under the counter.

He went to the stand he'd seen through the window. There were Ray-Ban-style plain shades that wouldn't look too bad. He tried them on, acting as if he was looking in the mirror. The resonances he picked up were confined to his hands and his taste-buds, but he didn't like to make any assumptions when it came to that stuff. The shades didn't seem to be hiding any nasty surprises. He took them off and headed to the counter.

The girl was still smiling in that strange, awkward way that made her appear nervous. He wondered how much she knew about what had happened to him. Was she afraid of him?

"Kind of dull for sunglasses outside," she said, flinching as the words left her mouth.

He shrugged. "Could brighten up later."

She rung them up, and he got his wallet out. He'd gotten used to opening it with his gloved hands, but he still felt weird doing it in front of anyone. Most normal people handled cash without them. He felt his face flush as he passed the money over. "Thanks."

She shrugged as he picked up his new protective eyewear. There was something in her expression that made him pause. She turned away quickly, opening a door behind the counter. Her eyes had seemed watery, like she'd been about to cry.

***

Bridget folded her arms. Her plan could be shot to shit if Zack got tangled up with his old girlfriend now. She'd just have to hope he was as hopeless around all women as he was around Cassandra.

He came out with a pair of sunglasses and started heading towards the exit. He glanced back at the shop once, but it was enough to make Bridget change up her strategy. She couldn't risk losing him to her. His crush on Cassandra was bad enough. At least, he seemed to realise that woman was out of his league. The last thing she needed was to lose him to the necromancer. Plan C was nowhere near as pleasant as Plan B. She shuddered as she followed him to the exit.

The sky was still grey, and the first droplets of rain were starting to fall. She stepped outside and hurried along. Zack stopped leading to follow her, seeming to realise she was sticking to shaded areas. The day was cloudy, but there were a few breaks in the coverage, and she didn't want to risk bursting into flames in the middle of the street.

"It's up here," Zack said, pointing out the street sign.

She already knew where it was. She could sense the

vampire now that she was close. This was why she'd been assigned to protect Zack. The necromancers could control the dead, but they couldn't sense them, not like she could. There was no way for them to know when vampires were in town. Bridget was Zack's first line of defence. He needed her. Almost as much as she needed him.

"She's awake," Bridget murmured. A conscious vampire was a deadly vampire. "Ready?"

Zack gulped. He put on the sunglasses he'd just bought. He nodded, but he smelled tastier suddenly. It was almost enough to trigger her fangs. She shook off the hunger and moved forward, towards the new vampire.

***

Chloe took a few calming breaths. It was the first time she'd spoken a word to Zack since the hospital. The first time, and it had all been meaningless small talk.

There was nothing else it could have been and she knew that, but that didn't make her feel any better. She bit at her lip. She had to forget him like he'd forgotten her.

The problem was, she wasn't sure she could. She looked down at the keys she had clutched in her hand. She could go to Larry's place and hopefully find out what had happened to him. She knew where he stayed now, from helping him make it back to his flat after Bridget had bitten him. She should at least check his place out, anyway. As much as she dreaded finding out what his fate had been, it came with the upside that it might actually take her mind off Zack.

She laughed as she moved out from behind the counter

and got her own keys out to close the shop. There wasn't a chance in hell that it might take her mind off him. Nothing had been able to do that. She knew the bitter truth, and it stung every time she was faced with it.

It would take a lot longer to erase Zack from her life than it had taken a single vampire to erase her from his.

CHAPTER TEN

Zack followed Bridget to the house. She walked with confidence, her hips swinging, gait long and even. Little tremors rippled over his skin. What if the girl really was a vampire? He shuddered. He was sure his arms must be covered in goose bumps under his clothes. He couldn't believe what they were about to do. He knew he wasn't exactly in any position to question anyone's sanity but this… this went beyond insanity.

"Wait," he said as they got to the front door. "What are we doing?"

She smiled. "Killing a vampire. What did you think we were doing?"

She knocked on the front door. Waited.

He swallowed. "What if… I mean, could this be considered murder?"

She laughed, a gentle noise that birthed baby goose bumps on top of his pre-existing goose bumps.

"You can't murder a dead person."

"What about… Don't vampires have rules about this kind of thing?"

Her smile tightened. "She's a direct threat to you, Zack. That makes her a staked vampire walking."

He tried not to think about it anymore. Bridget knew what she was doing. He was safe.

The door went unanswered. Bridget sighed, turned the handle. The door was locked.

"Oh, well," Zack said. "We should probably—"

Bridget did something to the door with her thin, girlish hand. Something snapped and it swung inwards. She looked at him. "Well, I hate to do this, but I need you to lure her out of the house."

"Uhn, what?"

"I can't walk in since I'm not invited. You have to get her to come outside."

"Eh, no." That was not happening. Not in a million years. He shook his head.

"She's hungry. You go inside, she'll smell you, and you'll just need to run back out here."

Like that made it sound any better. He looked into the house. It was dark, but everything was dark. His sunglasses had a downside. He still wasn't taking them off.

"Zack, I hate to ask," she said, sounding resigned. "But it's the only way. Listen, she'll be able to smell you if you just get a little bit closer. Just walk in to about that door there," she said, pointing inside. "Stand there for five seconds and then run right back out here."

He frowned. It didn't sound particularly hard, but he was freaking the hell out. Maybe if Bridget hadn't told him what the vampires wanted to do to him…

"She's new, Zack. She barely knows what she's doing. She'll just try to bite you," Bridget went on.

"Great," he muttered, trying to psych himself up.

Bridget came down a step and brushed his hair behind his ears. It was definitely getting a bit on the long side, but he hadn't been able to force himself to go and get it cut. Something about sitting still while some guy stood behind him with a pair of scissors made him queasy. He had no idea how he'd done it before the incident, but he knew he must have since it had been a lot shorter then.

Bridget apparently wasn't done touching him. He watched in surprise as she straightened up his shirt collar, a look in her eyes he'd never seen before. Did she actually like him? Was that even possible?

"You'll be fine. I'll make sure of it. Trust me, I don't want you getting hurt."

He was glad the sunglasses were there to hide his shock. Bridget had always been cool around him; she'd never shown any real sign of affection before. He'd assumed she didn't really like him or her assignment. He hadn't thought she could even separate the two.

"You know what I am now, Zack," she went on. "You know, and you trust me. Trust me when I say I'll burn up out here if you don't hurry up." She stepped back.

He rushed up the stairs, the realisation that Bridget was under threat for every second he hesitated making him panic. He needed her.

He darted into the house and stopped at the door she'd pointed out. Five seconds, she'd said. He counted them out slowly in his head, glancing around as he did so. He was waiting for a hungry, out-of-control vampire to come tearing out thirsting for his blood. He hoped to God the plan worked like Bridget thought it would.

The sound of a door banging open grabbed his attention as he got to 'four'. His head snapped around. The girl burst into the hallway, right in between him and his escape route. She wore only underwear and a shit-ton of blood. He stared, a scream trapped in his throat as she sniffed the air and grinned at him with blood-coated fangs.

Seeing the girl who'd dropped dead right in front of him standing there looking like a monster gave him uncontrollable shudders. It was too much to take in, and his escape route being blocked was cranking his fear up. Vampires were real. He couldn't deny that any longer. He fought to pull in a breath as his chest constricted in panic. He couldn't believe it. He just couldn't…

"Steve, man, you've got to help me! I just saw a vampire. I swear to God, I'm not taking the piss. She wanted to bite me. I'm never going to sleep again…"

"Zack, have you been taking your pills? Because it doesn't sound like you have."

"I need help. I can't keep having these visions. I took the pills. Maybe they don't work."

"What have I told you before? Vampires aren't real, Zack. Take deep breaths. Tap your neck."

"My neck?" He wondered why it felt so hot. It was like he was being tattooed or burned with a cigarette, over and over again.

"Tap it," Steve told him.

"I don't think I can move."

"Why can't you move?"

Zack blinked. The room came into focus and he realised the vampire was on top of him, her blood-stained body pinning him to the floor. The pain in his neck was her fangs. He could feel them inside him as she sucked his blood out of the wound they'd created.

He wasn't sure how long his mental break had lasted, but she sure as hell hadn't wasted any time getting her teeth into him. Shit! He pushed at her, hard. She didn't move, not a fraction of an inch. His head was fuzzy; blood loss, he supposed. He could hear something, though, someone making a racket close by, and when he finally managed to focus on it, he recognised Bridget's voice.

"Hey, Bitch," Bridget called out, her voice clear and demanding. "Get out here. I command you."

He pushed at the vampire again. She got up of her own accord, he assumed, since she moved swiftly and without further prompting. The pain of having her teeth extracted from his neck made his stomach heave. He rolled onto his side and puked onto the stranger's carpet. Blood spattered his vomit, pulsing out of his neck. He clamped his hand over the wound as he dragged himself up.

He saw the vampire rush at Bridget. Her crazy plan had at least worked. He'd console himself with that fact when he was bleeding less copiously or maybe after he died from the loss.

Bridget moved quickly, and Zack saw the girl go from a

blood-spattered, half-naked teenager to a mass of blackened, smoky-smelling dust. So that's what happened when vampires died? He got onto his knees, not quite steady enough to make it to his feet yet. His head was swimming as Bridget tried to get closer. He wondered why she wasn't rushing over to help him. Then he remembered. She couldn't get into the house; she hadn't been invited.

"Zack, you need to get over here. I can help you but you need to get over here, now!"

The helpless look in her eyes was unfamiliar and kind of terrifying.

He felt his eyes roll up in his head as he fell forward onto the carpet.

***

Witnessing this from the other side of the doorway, Bridget took her mobile out of her pocket and cursed as she waited for Kenny to pick up. She'd fucked up badly, and she needed help. Nothing she could do on her own would get Zack out of that goddamned house. Kenny was ignoring his phone or he was sleeping. She cursed again and realised he wasn't her best choice right now, anyway. Chloe would make a much better accomplice.

She dialled the girl's mobile number, having been given the contact details when she'd taken the job guarding Zack. Every necromancer in town had a place in her phone book. If she'd known which of the others was the closest, she might have called them. As it was, Chloe would need to do.

"What do *you* want?" the girl asked, pleasant as ever.

"Help," Bridget said. "Zack's been bitten. He's passed out. I can't get to him."

"Where are you?" Concern was now evident in her voice.

Bridget gave the address, smiling at the hint of anxiety in Chloe's tone as she repeated it back to her.

"I'm on my way."

Bridget hung up and glanced around. The bushes surrounding the house would have hidden her little scuffle with the newbie vamp. The neighbours didn't appear to be nosy. Or they were all out at work, more likely. She tried to contain her impatience, pacing and rearranging everything she touched from her hair to the buttons on her coat. Finally, she caught sight of the necromancer and was able to calm herself.

Chloe jumped out of a taxi, rushing towards her as the cab drew away.

"Where is—" Her eyes widened as her gaze moved past Bridget. She pushed her out of her way without a second's hesitation and ran into the house.

Chloe managed to get Zack to the threshold within a few seconds, dragging him out with her arms under his. He was still unconscious. She held him for a few seconds, lowering him to the ground and sitting with his head on her knees. She brushed back his hair and checked his pulse at his neck.

Bridget watched the panic fade from the necromancer's face as she confirmed her old lover's heart was still beating.

Chloe glowered at Bridget as she moved, cradling Zack's upper body until Bridget took hold of him herself. Chloe did her best not to touch her as she gave up her hold on

Zack. She swallowed as she got back to her feet.

Bridget hid a smirk as she got comfortable on the cold concrete path and pulled the unconscious human onto her lap. Chloe hovered over them, her gaze never moving from his face. It was just pathetic how much she still cared for him. Bridget licked his bite wound to heal it, savouring the taste of his blood and fighting the urge to drink from him. His pulse seemed steady. He hadn't lost too much. He'd be fine. As the tension drained out of her shoulders, she realised how worried she'd actually been.

"Is he okay?"

Chloe's clipped tone made her jump.

"He'll be fine," Bridget said, not looking up. He just looked like he was sleeping.

"You let this happen," Chloe said.

There was nothing Bridget could say to that, so she said nothing.

"The Council needs to know about this."

"Good luck with that," Bridget said, knowing Kenny would block Chloe's path.

"Bitch," Chloe spat out. "You let him get hurt again and I'll—"

"You'll what? Force me to obey your every word? Go ahead." She squeezed Zack's shoulder as he started to stir. "This won't happen again."

Chloe snorted. "If it does—"

"If it does, I'll be replaced," Bridget snapped. "You've served your purpose here. You can leave."

Chloe glared at her. Her gaze fell to Zack, and Bridget

knew she'd succeeded in torturing the girl by bringing her here.

"If anything happens to him, I'll kill you myself." Chloe then walked away.

Bridget watched her go and wondered what exactly she was going to report to her superiors. Either way, she was going to have to call Rick, and soon.

Zack groaned. "What the…"

He sat up swiftly, grimacing and rubbing at his head with one of his gloved hands. "What happened?"

Bridget got to her feet as a sudden breeze stirred up the dead vampire's remains at her feet and the black ash swirled upwards. "You were bitten. I need to get you home."

He stumbled as she helped him to his feet. "My head is kind of fuzzy…"

"You lost a little blood."

He shuddered, but he didn't speak as she guided him away from the house.

If the close call had shown her anything, it was that Zack was weaker than she'd thought. She wondered if he was really worth saving at this point. He'd had another episode when the vampire had attacked him. He was so broken inside, she wasn't sure how much was even left to salvage.

He moaned softly, rubbing at his neck as he pulled away from her. She let him stagger alongside her without touching him. Her hand went into her pocket, fingers brushing her phone. She really needed to speak to Rick.

***

Chloe walked to Larry's flat, where she'd been headed before Bridget sidetracked her with the curveball from hell. What the hell had happened out there, exactly? She'd been too pissed to stay and ask questions and too afraid to see Zack wake up and look at her the same way he had the morning after his original attack.

She chewed on her bottom lip as she tried to think of something she could do to keep Zack safe from the vampire bitch who'd been assigned to protect him. She'd never trusted Bridget, and she never would. Wild animals couldn't ever really be tamed. Something would set her off. Zack would never be safe around her.

The location snuck up on her. She realised she'd walked past the flat after a few aimless seconds passed. The building was four storeys tall and looked new. The door remained wedged open because of a little girl's bike stuck in there. Larry wouldn't even need to know she was on her way up. The element of surprise was probably a good thing, considering she didn't know what kind of state she'd find him in.

She went into the corridor and shivered. The day hadn't been particularly warm, but the hallway struck her as icy-cold and kind of dark. She glanced up; the lights were off. Taking the stairs two at a time, she made her way to Larry's flat.

The keys in her hand weren't just keys to the arcade. She was assuming the others were to the flat and his car. They might not be, but right now it didn't matter. Finding out what had happened to him was what she'd come here for.

She raised her fist to knock and thought better of it. Announcing her arrival might not be the best idea. Her hand fell to the doorknob. It turned, and the door opened when she pushed it. The dark hallway smelled of smoke. She took a step inside and closed the door quietly.

The floorboards creaked lightly as she moved, making her wince with every carefully placed step. She really hoped she wasn't about to catch the teenager doing anything weird. Pausing outside a closed door, she asked herself what the hell she thought she was doing. Doubt crept in. Larry was probably fine. What would he think if he found her in his flat? She groaned.

A creaking inside the room made her freeze in place. *Shit.*

"Chloe?" He sounded dazed, as if he'd just woken up.

She should just drop his keys and run, but something didn't feel right. She had to make sure he was okay. Swallowing, she pulled herself together and forced a smile.

"Larry, are you okay?" Her voice sounded a bit shaky, but she managed to take a step forward and push at the door gently.

His hand caught the edge and pulled the door open all the way. Her gaze found his surprisingly muscular and entirely hairless naked chest and she struggled to force it upwards to take in his face. A gasp fell from her lips as she saw the change in his skin and hair. The acne was gone, his hair shiny without looking greasy. His blue eyes seemed brighter against the prettier background. He had thick eyelashes. She hadn't even noticed that before. Good bone structure, too. She bit her lip. Asking him if he was okay right now seemed like a stupid question.

"I'm fine," he said, smiling brightly.

She'd had no idea how cute he could look when he smiled. Larry was actually hot. Who would have guessed? She blinked and tried to think straight. This wasn't the awkward teenager who liked pushing his luck with her and every other girl under thirty in the arcade. He'd never gotten a date from any of them. Somehow, she didn't think that was going to be a problem for him anymore.

"Uh, Larry, how are you feeling right now?" She supposed she had to deal with the reality of the situation sooner or later.

"I feel great," he said, stretching and drawing attention to his newly developed muscles.

Her gaze dropped and she shook her head.

"I can see that." She jingled his keys. "I found these in the arcade. Someone broke in last night."

His face dropped. "Shit. Am I fired? What happened?"

"What happened to you last night, Larry?"

He frowned. "I… don't remember."

She concentrated to confirm her suspicions, gazing into his pretty blue eyes. "Repeat after me, 'I am Larry, and I am a vampire'."

He gazed at her slackly for a second before he spoke in a toneless voice. "I am Larry, and I am a vampire." He blinked. "Wait. What?"

She sighed. "You're dead."

"I am?"

She nodded, wishing he didn't look so good. Vampirism had its benefits, she supposed.

Confusion clouded his expression, making him even cuter than he'd been before.

"Have you looked into a mirror lately by any chance?"

He shook his head, his eyes widening. "What are you saying? Do I not have a reflection now?"

He started to move out of the room when he seemed to realise she was blocking his path. There must have been something in her gaze because he stopped and stared back, his new sexy body inches from hers.

"I *knew* you liked me."

He didn't wait for her to confirm or deny it; he just dipped his head down and kissed her on the lips.

She kissed back on reflex. His mouth opened wider as his lips worked against hers. She pushed him back when his saliva made the skin around her mouth wet.

Wiping at her mouth, she frowned at him. "That so wasn't…"

He cringed. "Sorry. I don't know what I was—"

"Wait," she said, placing her hand on his chest.

His heart wouldn't pump blood until he drank some. That weird technicality was what allowed vampires to have a sex life. She scrubbed the thought from her head. She wasn't so attention-starved that she'd jump into bed with Larry, even if he was sexy as hell now. "You won't get anywhere with girls if that's how you kiss."

"Girls?" He looked crestfallen. "But I thought *you* liked me. I'm sorry I kissed you. I should have asked you out first, but you always say no… Well, not *no*. You always say you're doing something else. But…"

"Larry, shut up and pay attention." She slipped an arm around his neck and brought his lips to hers. The impulsive decision to straighten out his technique had nothing to do with how desperate she was getting for physical contact. At least, that was what she was telling herself.

He immediately started to do the same thing he'd done before, and she broke away.

"Don't try to cover my whole mouth with yours. It feels weird."

She didn't wait for him to say anything else—she just pressed her lips to his again and he let her lead him into the kind of kiss she really wanted, slowly and softly. It made her heart rate spike being so close to a man like this. It had been more than six months since…

"Wow," he said with a sigh when she withdrew.

"Now, that's how you kiss a girl." She folded her arms as she stepped back.

What was she thinking? Their first kiss should never even have happened. The second one had been pushing it. Larry gazed at her dreamily, and she felt her face flush. It would be far too easy to use Larry to make her forget about Zack. As tempting as it was, she didn't have those kinds of feelings for him and she'd only end up hurting him.

"You know I'm like, in love with you, right?"

She smiled. He was too young to know what love really was. Now that he'd morphed into a total hottie overnight, she guessed he wouldn't be a stranger to it for much longer. She ignored the infatuation in his eyes. "You've got far bigger problems right now."

"Far bigger… Oh, right. I'm a vampire?"

She nodded. "Right. You'll be getting hungry soon, and it's not exactly legal for a newly hatched vampire to be without a guardian."

"What's a guardian?"

She sighed. It was going to be a long night. "Just go take a shower and check the mirror. I'll be back soon with your dinner."

He beamed, and she could practically tell what he was thinking before he spoke.

"Dinner? So this is like a date."

She didn't bother to correct him, just concentrated as they locked eyes. "You will not leave this flat until I say so."

"I will not leave this flat until you say so." He shook his head. "Man, you're bossy."

She managed a wry smile as she headed for the door. "You don't know the half of it."

CHAPTER ELEVEN

Zack lay in bed, wondering if he'd imagined Bridget's tearful eyes as she'd told him what exactly had happened. The vampire attack had come back to him, bit by bit, after he'd regained consciousness. He wished that had happened the first time he'd woken up disoriented after a traumatic event, even though his mental state apparently hadn't been able to take it as all the doctors who'd diagnosed his amnesia had told him. So much for second opinions; he'd had four of them singing from the same hymn sheet.

He sighed. He was shattered and weak, and sick of not knowing why he was under protection.

Bridget came into his room with a tray. She seemed short with her heels off, but he supposed it could also be because he was lying down. He sat up, looking at the tray and not really wanting any of the food. It didn't matter that he'd bought the cookies from Cassandra. Right now, the thought of eating anything made his stomach turn.

"It'll help," she said, putting the tray on the bedside table. "The sugar, I mean, with the blood loss."

He hid his gloved hands under the covers, knowing how weird it would look. He'd reluctantly removed the sunglasses when they got into the house, but he wasn't in any kind of state to remove the gloves. Shivering at the thought, he smiled weakly at his nurse.

"Thanks."

She sat down next to him. "You know I would die for you, Zack."

He stared at her. "Is someone asking you to?"

She smiled. "No. It's just something that could happen. I'm here to protect you at all costs. I wasn't sure I could do it, not at first, but…" She took a breath he was sure she didn't need. "I started to see how much you needed me, and I got to like working with you. I would die for you now, and it wouldn't be out of duty." She leaned forward and brushed his hair out of his face. "You should get some rest."

"Are you going to stay tonight?" He didn't feel so weird about asking after her admission. She actually liked him? He never would have guessed it.

She nodded. "I'll be in the other room if you need anything."

He thought about asking her to share his bed, but he was tired as hell and she was too quick to leave the room to allow him the chance. Knowing she'd be close by to protect him while he slept was enough to make his body stop fighting his exhaustion.

***

Bridget went into the kitchen to call Rick. Zack wouldn't hear her. He'd likely pass out soon, and if he wasn't tired, the sleeping pills she'd crushed into his milk would help him along. She tapped her nails off his tiny kitchen table as she waited for her boss to answer. He let it ring almost a dozen times.

"Bridget?"

"The Winter Clan know where Zack is. They sent someone."

He sucked in a breath. "What happened?"

"I dealt with it. Relax. I need to know what to tell the FBU. We need damage control."

"Damage control," he murmured.

She rolled her eyes. As usual, she was going to have to work out what to do on her own.

"Tell them nothing," he said.

"If Winter keep sending vampires—"

"Inform me if they do. I'm going to make some calls."

"I've got a check-in coming up, Rick. If they think Zack isn't safe with me—"

"When is the check-in?"

"Next week."

"How's Plan B coming?"

"It's been started. Might be a slow burner. He's one of those shy types."

She cringed at the thought of doing anything sexual with him. Not to mention that Kenny would bash Zack's brains in if he even suspected anything was going on between them. The thought made her shiver in delight. Her lover's primal side was one of the reasons she kept going back to him.

Rick made a 'hmm' noise. "Should we skip that stage?"

"No," she said quickly. "It's essential. Your instincts were right. This is what he needs to blind-side him."

"Keep me up to date with it. If the FBU gets in contact, let me know."

She agreed and hung up. She had one week to make Zack think she was in love with him. One week to execute the plan. She tapped her nails off the table. As soon as Zack was asleep, she'd head next door.

CHAPTER TWELVE

Larry was naked on the couch when Chloe came back with a bag of butcher shop blood. He grinned at her, though his eyes didn't meet hers when he looked up. She closed her eyes, mostly to stop them from wandering.

"You said not to leave. You didn't say not to be naked."

She heard him move and opened her eyes, stepping back as he made to kiss her. She held out a hand.

"I'm not over Zack," she said sharply. "So don't go thinking we've got something just because I showed you how to kiss a girl properly."

He frowned, and she got the distinct impression that he knew she was attracted to him now.

She cursed inwardly. "Never should have told you to check a mirror."

"You kissed back, the first time, I mean," he said, covering his private parts with his hands. He glanced down. "Anyway, I don't think my dick works right anymore. I couldn't get more than a semi in the shower. I just kind of wanted to check…"

She rolled her eyes. "Okay, here's the deal. You're a vampire now. That means you died. Which means your heart doesn't beat, which means your blood isn't getting pumped around your body, which means your man parts don't work like they used to."

"Aw, man," he said. "This is like the only time I was ever getting a chance to get laid and I can't?"

"You had no chance of getting laid," she told him, starting to regret the kiss.

"That's not what I meant. I meant I look okay now."

"You look hot now," she corrected, catching his smile and trying not to encourage it. "And I'm not saying you can't get laid. I'm saying you need this to get your heart going, and that's the only way you'll be able to, you know…"

His eyes widened. "What is it?"

"Clothes first." She stepped back from the doorway, and he darted to his room.

A minute later, he came out in jeans and a T-shirt that hid his new drool-inducing physique. She breathed a sigh of relief. The last thing she needed was a fling with a nineteen-year-old vampire. Controlling herself around him wasn't going to be easy. It had been so long since she'd kissed a guy, let alone… She shook her head. She was so not a cougar.

"So what is it?" He looked at the bag.

"Blood, what else?"

He screwed up his nose. "Oh, right."

"Come on, there are different kinds. You can see what kind you like best."

"Kinds?"

"You know, pig, cow, sheep."

"Enticing," he murmured. "So can I still eat real food?"

She shook her head. "You're on a liquid diet now."

His kitchen was a typical single guy's dumping ground. She eyed the pile of unwashed dishes.

"I was going to do those later," he defended himself, clamping the lid down on the dirty washing basket as he passed.

She smiled. The basket was full. He was probably wearing the only clean clothes he had left. She put the bag down on his newspaper-covered table. "Okay, so you can heat these in the microwave or you can drink it cold. I've heard it tastes better warm."

"Can you try it with me?"

"Uh, no," she said, realising he was as grossed out by thought as she was.

"Why? Don't you…" he trailed off as his eyes lit with understanding. "Oh! You don't drink the animal stuff, then?"

"Of course not. Wait. What do you mean?"`

"Well, you're a vampire, too, right? That's why you know all this stuff."

She took a breath. "I'm not a vampire. I know this stuff because I'm a necromancer. I can control the dead."

He stared at her. "So how did I become a vampire if you didn't bite me?"

"A vampire bit you. He's dust now. You're on your own. I came to find you because the vampire who bit you left your keys in the arcade."

"What was he doing at the arcade? Did he try to hurt you?"

"No. It's a long story."

It would be a mistake to tell him about Zack. She couldn't be sure another vampire wouldn't show up and claim Larry as theirs. If he knew about Zack, he could be a danger to him. She'd tried to make herself bring a stake back instead of blood, but she hadn't been able to face killing her friend. Larry hadn't become one of the undead on purpose. He'd been made. He didn't deserve to have his existence cut short.

"So which is which?" He poked at the bag.

She took out the bags of blood. Tiny little bits of bone and other gross-looking shit floated in the red liquid. She fought a shudder and asked if he had a strainer. He started searching his cupboards. By the time they'd heated up some pig's blood for him to try, she was swearing off meat for life.

"Bottoms up," he said and then picked up the mug and took a sip.

She expected him to blanch, but after that first taste hit his tongue, he seemed reluctant to put the mug back down. She watched him drain it and then lick at the inside of the mug. If he hadn't been so cute, it might have been creepy, especially when he put it down and she saw the little slashes of blood at either side of his mouth.

"I need more," he said, picking up the mug of cold cow's blood and draining it at the same speed. "Hot is better." He shrugged, his tongue flicking out to catch the blood staining the corners of his mouth. "But *fuck me*, that was good."

"Glad you liked it. I'll get more. You'll need to drink about the same amount every day."

She was glad he'd actually enjoyed it. It would be easier to keep him from wanting to try human blood. Not that she'd be the one to keep him in line. She bit at her lip. Kenny would road-block her, as usual, if she tried to go through him. It would be best if he didn't know.

"Damn," she whispered, knowing what it meant. She'd have to be Larry's guardian until she turned thirty. She'd be deemed fully trained by then. She'd have the chance to call the Council herself.

"Any kind," Larry said, looking at the other bags. "They're different, but in a good way."

She nodded. "There are a few things you'll need to know to get by."

"Like what?"

"Well, for one thing, you won't want to spend too much time in the sun," she said, then seeing understanding light up his expression.

"Oh. Oh, right. I'm a vampire."

"Yeah, so, good points include instant hotness, super strength and speed, and immortality. Bad points include an aversion to direct sunlight, holy objects, and the possibility of being tracked down by the clan who made you. There aren't many rogue vampires out there. Most of them join the FBU—"

"The FBU?"

"It's kind of like the vampire police," she said with a shrug.

He grinned. "Cool! How do I sign up?"

"That's going to have to wait," she told him, wondering what the hell she was doing. "You need to be proved stable by your guardian before they'll let you in."

"So you're my guardian, right?"

She nodded slowly, hoping she wasn't going to regret the decision. Council rules dictated she should hand him over to Kenny to let the Elders decide his fate and his guardian, but he didn't deserve to go through an unsympathetic guardian who wouldn't speak up for him to the Elders, and she really didn't want to have to call that arsehole if she didn't absolutely need to.

"Awesome." He put his hands on his hips. "So, now that I've had blood…"

"I'm not going to sleep with you." She shook her head.

He shrugged. "Can't blame a guy for trying."

CHAPTER THIRTEEN

Kenny lay back against the pillows, a satisfied smile spreading over his face. He wrapped his arms around Bridget, and she laid her head against his chest. The pounding of his heart made her hungry, even though he'd already let her taste his blood while they had fun. She was starting to salivate when she heard something louder and far more alarming. Her phone was ringing from her jacket pocket across the room. She moved, and Kenny tightened his grasp on her.

"Hey," she said. "I have to get that."

"You don't have to do anything," he whispered.

She shivered as her body obeyed his command.

"I have a job to do," she reminded him. "I could be removed from this assignment if I mess it up."

He sighed and let her go. "I just want one full night with you. Is that so much to ask?"

She moved away, leaving him to whine about the unfairness of it all as she picked up her phone and dress and left the room.

"I just got word about the FBU's visit," Rick said, skipping pleasantries as she picked up his call.

"Uh, I told you about that. We have a week."

"You have three days. They're concerned. Someone started a rumour."

Her grip on the phone tightened. A rumour? "What are you talking about?"

She wished he wouldn't be so scant with his details. Stage-whispering everything he said was annoying enough.

"I'm talking about Winter. The FBU received an anonymous tip that you joined their clan."

She frowned. "This had better be a joke. It's not funny, Rick. You of all people should—"

"It's no joke," he hissed.

She swallowed. Someone was treading dangerously close to the truth. Her clan affiliations were well-hidden: she wasn't marked by Midnight because she had to be beyond reproach by the FBU, and a clan branding would be an easy way to expose her. That didn't mean her bosses couldn't suspect her for being in a clan. If they suspected Winter, they thought she was part of that clan's apparent plan to capture Zack. She cursed under her breath. Things were spiralling out of her control. "The plan needs to be accelerated, then."

"We need to skip ahead to Plan C."

"I've got three days?"

"You should be timing your exit strategy a bit tighter than that."

"You want me to do this within the next forty-eight hours?"

"I wouldn't say no."

***

Chloe left Kenny a voicemail to get him to tell the Council she'd taken guardianship of a new vampire. She seriously doubted he would actually get back to her if he even listened to the message, but she'd at least have done her part to process the request. It hadn't been an easy decision, but she figured she wouldn't be breaking any rules if she at least left him that message. If he called her back, she could ignore the call. Considering how easily he usually ignored her, it seemed like the right choice.

She sighed as she made her way back to the shop. The arcade would close soon. She wondered why she was even bothering as she walked into the building.

Cassandra was locking up her cafe as she walked by. The woman turned.

"Oh, Chloe! Have you seen Zack today? He wasn't around when I brought his lunch, and it isn't like him…"

Chloe bit back a snarky retort. The woman was as innocent as they came. She couldn't help but roll her eyes before she turned to face her. "He went home sick. I'm sure he'll be back tomorrow."

She glanced at the bag in Cassandra's hand as the woman proffered it. "Can you take this to him? I wouldn't want it to go to waste."

Chloe took in her smile and snatched the bag out of her hand. Her fingers brushed Cassandra's smooth skin, and she fought back a shiver. This was why she hated interacting with the woman. There was something off about her, something not quite human. She wasn't a necromancer, and she wasn't a vampire. Whatever she was, she always felt weird.

"I suppose," Chloe muttered.

Cassandra thanked her and left the arcade. She shook her head as she walked to her shop, half a mind to toss the damn thing in the bin. The thought of Zack left alone with that vampire made her stop and re-think things. He'd been hurt. Bridget might take advantage of that.

As much as she wanted to walk away and not look back, she knew she couldn't do that. The sandwich gave her an excuse to visit him, to see if he was really okay after he'd been attacked.

Every necromancer in town knew where Zack lived now that he'd been moved to a flat in the middle of Shady Pines. She headed out without giving it any more thought. Her nerves disappeared as her worry grew. Checking in on him would put her mind at rest.

***

Zack got up and went to the bathroom. A glance into the living room showed him that Bridget had left. Panic began to swell in his chest. He couldn't deal with being alone right now.

He rushed to dress, hoping a walk outside would calm him. There was every chance he'd have one of his weird episodes if he went out alone and didn't calm down, but it was a risk he was willing to take if there was even the slightest chance it might relax him. He shoved the sunglasses on once his shoes were laced.

The knock on the door made him jump. What if this was it? What if they'd come for him?

Don't be stupid, he told himself. A vampire wouldn't knock. That was far too polite. He didn't usually get visitors, though. So who the hell was at the door?

He moved forward slowly, not quite willing to take the sunglasses off. He didn't want to make it easy for them. A second knock came as he put his gloved hand on the knob. He turned it and yanked it inwards.

The girl from the shop where he'd bought the sunglasses was staring at him, a bag from Cassandra's cafe in her hand. She smiled tightly.

"Hi. Cassandra asked me to drop this off. She was worried since you weren't around for lunch."

"Oh. Right. Thanks," he said, wondering when he'd stopped being able to form proper sentences.

"Are you okay?"

He took the bag from her and took the sunglasses off with his other hand. He winced at the rustle of the bag as his gloved hand closed around it. The girl already thought he was off. Why did he have to be wearing sunglasses when he answered the door?

He somehow managed to turn a grimace into a smile.

"I was just going out, that's why I was—"

"It's just started to rain," she said, smiling in that way he knew was meant for humouring someone strange.

"Oh. I hadn't noticed. I don't think I have an umbrella."

"Then maybe you should stay in. Bridget said you lost some blood earlier. You should rest."

"You know Bridget?"

He winced as he said it. Of course, she knew Bridget. She worked in the arcade. It was the blood loss he should have asked about. Did knowing about that mean the girl was one of the necromancers Bridget had told him about?

"I know a lot of people," she said, folding her arms. "Anyway, I should get going."

"Wait," he said. "You're not wearing a jacket. Come in and wait out the rain."

He knew he sounded desperate. He just hoped he didn't sound creepy. Being with a stranger wouldn't be as bad as being alone.

Surprise widened her eyes. "Uhm…"

"I know we don't know each other, but I don't bite. I promise not to try anything inappropriate."

He was making things worse, so he shut his stupid mouth.

She smiled, and it looked warm but wry. "Make me a cup of tea, and I'll take my chances."

"Done," he said, letting her in and closing the door behind her.

He led the way to the kitchen, keeping his mouth shut to avoid saying anything else that might send her running for the exit.

He put the sandwich into the fridge and put the kettle on as she settled into one of the hard wooden kitchen chairs. He watched her glance around the room, dark eyes curious under her long fringe as she took in the small space. A whisper of a smile passed across her face. He wondered what she was thinking, noticed he was staring and tried harder to keep his attention on making the tea.

She cleared her throat and glanced his way. "So, have you lived here long?"

"About six months."

He got mugs out of the cupboard, realising she was his second ever visitor, after Bridget. He wondered where Bridget had gone. It seemed odd that she'd leave after everything that had happened. She was probably coming back.

"You like it here?"

"It's okay," he said, shrugging as he put teabags into the cups. He knew the girl would find it weird that he was still wearing the gloves, but he couldn't quite make himself take them off. "How long have you worked in the arcade?"

"Eight years, give or take."

He poured the tea and got out the milk and sugar. "You like it here?"

"I do," she said, taking the mug he put in front of her and smiling at it.

He'd left the teabag in there with a spoon. He put a tea-plate down and she fished the bag out and ditched it on there, watching him do the same before she poured milk into her mug.

"You don't like it sweet," he said, memorising the way she took her tea.

"I'm more of a bitter kind of person," she said with a wry smile.

"Life's a bitch," he said.

"And then you die," she added.

He smiled. He was starting to feel better already.

***

Bridget could hear Zack and Chloe talking when she finally left the comfort of Kenny's flat. It was an unwelcome development, and one she hadn't seen coming.

She slipped her shoes on and considered her options. Rick was right; she had to move quickly or it would all be over for them. Six months of careful planning would go straight down the drain. The wait for the FBU to back off and leave her to guard Zack on her own had taken the longest time. Any hint of unprofessional behaviour would have had her removed. She'd stuck it out. She'd been left alone with him, and her plan had just started to roll out. And now? She'd be damned if she was going to let him get away.

Collateral damage was inevitable. She had to move fast.

She opened the door and went into his flat. "Zack?"

"In here," he called out from the kitchen.

She walked in to find him sitting at his tiny kitchen table with his ex-girlfriend. She smiled sweetly at Chloe. The girl wasn't getting to mess things up.

"Chloe, how are you?"

Chloe frowned at her. "Funny. I was about to ask you the same thing."

"I'm fine, and Zack needs to get his rest."

"I feel okay," Zack said, shrugging.

Bridget was glad Plan B was being bypassed. Seducing

the guy wouldn't have been any fun. Taking him away from Chloe would be.

She smiled. "All the same. Visiting hours are over."

Chloe got up and glanced back at Zack. "I need to talk to Bridget for a second."

Bridget folded her arms. She refused to move until Chloe commanded her to. The hallway wasn't ideal, but Chloe hadn't wanted Zack to hear what she had to say, clearly.

"I don't know what you think you're doing, but you shouldn't be here," Bridget snapped once they were out of his earshot. "He's unstable. Trying to make him remember will only—"

Fire burned in Chloe's eyes. "I'm not trying to make him remember anything."

"It'll be your fault if he has a breakdown."

"You will not bite him," Chloe commanded. "You won't drink from him. You won't hurt him in any way…"

Bridget's anger rose with each command. Her thirst for human blood became undeniable. She launched herself at the necromancer who stopped her with a single word command.

"Stop." Chloe glared at her. "You are not hungry. You will drink your usual allowance of animal blood, and that is all."

"You don't own me," she snapped.

"Say goodnight to Zack for me." Chloe stalked away down the stairwell.

Bridget turned and punched the wall. The cracked concrete wasn't nearly as satisfying as draining Chloe dry would be. She flexed her scraped fingers, watching them heal before she went inside.

Chloe's command would hinder the new plan. She would have to circle back around to Plan B.

***

Zack cleared away the table, glad that he'd invited the girl in. He'd realised he hadn't gotten her name when Bridget had said it out loud. *Chloe.* Softer than he'd have guessed for someone with such a spiky personality. Still, he'd liked her. And she hadn't mentioned his gloves once.

He got the distinct impression Bridget didn't like her at all. He looked at the vampire as she came back into the room, alone.

"Chloe had to go," Bridget said, a tight smile fixed in place.

He rolled his eyes as he loaded the dishwasher. "She wasn't a threat."

"She isn't a vampire," Bridget told him. "That doesn't mean she isn't a threat."

"Someone sounds jealous," he joked. There was something weird between Bridget and Chloe. Since Bridget wasn't up for talking about it, he settled for taking the piss.

She sighed deeply and he turned, closing the door to the dishwasher and straightening.

"You don't know how hard it's been," Bridget said. She looked pained.

He frowned. "How hard what's been?"

"We spend every day together, Zack. Don't tell me you haven't noticed."

He stared at her, trying to wrap his head around what she was saying. "Noticed…?"

"This isn't easy for me." She clasped her hands together. "I like you, Zack. I'm sworn to protect you, so I shouldn't be feeling like this. It's just… it's wrong."

He blinked. She couldn't be saying what he thought she was. There'd been no indication of it up until now. Until some other girl started paying him attention. He tried not to roll his eyes at that little revelation. He could believe Bridget was being pissy that he was attracted to someone else but not out of any kind of feelings for him. She was more likely to be irritable that he wasn't lusting after her exclusively, not that he had ever looked at her that way, but she was very pretty and she damn well knew it. She had a problem with Cassandra, too, one that seemed based on how incredibly attractive she was. This wasn't a new look on her. She didn't like other women. He didn't know why he was even giving it a second thought.

"I'm kind of tired," he said, feeling his face flush at the lie.

"I'll go," she said. "Just, think about what I said. I'll see you in the morning."

***

Chloe walked home fuming. She kicked off her shoes when she got inside, letting out a frustrated growl. Technically, Bridget was right. She shouldn't have spoken to Zack at all. He was fragile right now; he didn't need her around. He didn't remember her, and she didn't want to go through the whole getting to know each other process again. Things wouldn't turn out the same way they had the first time. Everything was different now. He wasn't the same guy she'd fallen for.

She sighed. Maybe Larry wasn't such a bad idea…

"Shit," she swore, picking up her phone. She didn't know Larry's number, and she sighed again, heavier this time. Hauling her Doc Martens back on, she headed out. Babysitting wasn't on her top five list of favourite things, but it would be a distraction, at least.

She walked around to his flat and knocked on the door. He was talking inside, and she frowned as she strained to listen. Was he with a woman in there? She realised he wasn't when he opened the door, his phone in one hand. He ushered her in, and she tore her eyes away from his naked chest. The unbuttoned dress-shirt and smart trousers told her he was heading out. She folded her arms, leaning against the wall as he finished up his phone call.

"Aw, come on, Amira, you know you want to," he said, a smile on his face and earnestness in his tone.

Chloe raised an eyebrow at him. He shook his head and walked down the hall.

"Well, okay. But you should come next time. I'll buy you a drink."

He'd barely hung up when Chloe's phone vibrated in her pocket. She took it out and smiled. Amira had sent her text. She wondered what that could be about.

Larry was thankfully buttoning up his shirt when she looked up at him again.

"Well, that didn't go so well," he said.

"What, propositioning every girl in your phone book?"

He laughed. "Nah. Not exactly."

"Hey, Amira's a friend of mine. I don't want you—"

"I knew it. You do like me."

She rolled her eyes. "That's not what I'm saying here." She took a breath. "Anyway…what are you doing?"

"I'm going out."

"What for?"

"For a drink with friends."

"Uh, no, you're not." She shook her head. "This vampire thing is new, Larry. You need to get used to some things before you go out into warm nightclubs full of unsuspecting humans."

His face fell. "You're serious."

"Deadly," she said, going into her phone book. "I need your numbers. I can't be over here all the time, but I'll need to check in daily."

"So when am I okay to go for a night out, then?" He sounded whiny.

"A few weeks, maybe," she said, shrugging.

He sighed, sinking to the floor and pulling at his hair. "I finally have a shot with girls like Amira, and you're telling me I have to wait?"

Chloe stifled a snort of laughter. She sat down on crossed legs across from him. "You have to wait a few weeks *now*, but you'll have a lifetime to take your shot at those girls, Larry."

He glanced up. "A lifetime?"

"Unless you get staked or something," she joked, killing her smile when he grimaced at her. "You're going to look that good for a long time. Get used to it."

He grinned at the realization. Then it sank, just a little. "I just drank like four pints of blood. I thought I was maybe getting… *y'know* tonight."

"If that's a hint, you already know what my answer is. You'll just have to…" She made a tugging motion with her hand, and he sighed. "Now, give me your phone numbers."

She passed him her phone and he started to punch the details in.

She leaned against the wall and bit back a yawn. Her day had been long enough as it was. The thought of sticking around to make sure Larry behaved himself made her wince. She just wanted to get a cup of tea and go to bed.

"So…" Larry handed the phone back and straightened against the wall. "I know Zack lost all of his memories, but why does that mean you have to stay away from him?"

She smiled sadly. "He doesn't remember ever meeting me. I'm just a girl who works in the arcade. And he's just a guy who needs to be protected from the vampires who tried to kill him. Bridget is basically his bodyguard. I don't trust her."

She wasn't sure why she was telling Larry, but it felt good to unload.

"But what can I do?" She shrugged. "I'm nothing to him now."

"Wow," Larry said quietly. "Vampires tried to kill him? Why?"

His big eyes were curious.

She knew she could trust him. Even if he was a potential threat now, he wasn't part of a clan, and she would do everything she could to keep him away from that. If he ever became a real threat, she'd deal with him. She had power over him. Still, she hesitated to answer. The vampire who'd made Larry had come to Shady Pines for Zack.

"Because of what he can do."

"What? The guess-the-owner-of-the-trinket stuff? I thought that was like a carnival trick. I mean, I've seen him do it. It's creepy as shit. But it's fake, right?"

She shook her head, smiling wanly.

"It's not fake. He has…gifts." She knew he'd never seen it that way, but it's what they were. "It's up to the necromancers in town to protect him. Bridget's here because the FBU wanted to do some damage control and because necromancers can't actually track vampires." She shook her head. "There are necromancers all over town. No vampire in his right mind would come here. Rumour has it, Bridget was the only one they could get to volunteer to come here."

Larry stared at her, raptly. "They're afraid to come here?"

"You want a demonstration of why?" She smiled as he nodded. "Take your shirt off, Larry. Now."

His fingers went straight to the buttons, undoing them quickly.

She gave him just enough time to catch on that he had no real control against her demand. "Wait. Button it back up."

His fingers moved just as quickly as they had before. He

stared at her when he dropped his hands to his sides. "Weird."

"There are worse things a necromancer can order a vampire to do."

"Obviously," he said, folding his arms. "So, how many of those necromancers are there in town?"

"A lot."

"Like half the town a lot or one on every street a lot?"

"Try, generations of families who've lived here since the town was built. More than half the town if you need to put it that way. It might be a small place, but there are a lot of us."

He shuddered. "What happens when they find out about me?"

"I'm your guardian, Larry. No one's going to hurt you. You can relax."

He blew out a breath. "Wait. What about Amira?"

It took her a second to realise what he meant. "Her family only moved here when she was a kid, so no. She's not one of them."

He rubbed at his face. "This is crazy."

"And it's also late," Chloe said, getting to her feet and stretching. "Try to relax. Stay inside. I'll come back tomorrow with more blood."

She didn't make it sound like a command, but she made sure she looked him in the eye when she told him to stay inside.

"Okay," he said, nodding slowly. He didn't get up from where he sat, slumped against the wall in defeat.

She went outside and breathed in the cool night air. Another buzz from her pocket made her check and actually read Amira's text messages. She had to smile. The girl was clearly in shock, and whether it was because of Larry's newfound confidence or just because she didn't realise he fancied her, Chloe had no idea. She sent a message back, trying not to be too discouraging while also reminding herself Amira had no idea that vampires were real.

The reply she got back was non-committal. She didn't think she had anything to worry about.

***

Zack lay awake, wanting to pretend everything was normal—as normal as it could get with him—but the thought of creatures like the girl in that house coming for him proved enough to make him hellishly paranoid. He wanted to trust Bridget, but knowing she was one of them was enough to put the brakes on anything that might have otherwise happened between them. He wanted to believe she had some sort of feelings for him, but it didn't make any kind of sense. He wished she were human. It would take away the lingering doubts he still had about her.

"Damn it, Zack. You can't trust her," Audrey said with a sigh. "Why do guys always let the head with no brain win?"

"I'm kind of busy right now," he told her. "Can you call back later?"

She snorted. "Busy? Right. And I'm the chosen one."

"What do you want, then?"

"I want you to wake up and smell the vampire."

He sat upright in the bed. "What did you just say?"

"You heard me. You can't trust vampires. Not even the sexy ones who tell you they're into you. Especially not her."

"How do you know about vampires? This isn't funny, Audrey."

"Am I making a joke here? No. I don't think so. Don't let her fool you. She's out to get you."

He swallowed, not sure what to say to that. His big sister had tapped right into his own fears and laid them out for him to see. He was lucky he still had eyeballs, he supposed.

"What do I do?"

He hoped to hell she had some sort of advice. Thoughts of carrying around a crucifix and bathing in garlic made him cringe.

"You find something long and sharp. It doesn't have to be wooden. And you give her the long kiss goodnight. Threat eliminated."

He let himself fall back onto the bed. "Thanks a million. I never would have thought of that on my own."

"She'll finish the job they started, little Z. She wasn't lying about the things they would have done to you."

"Hey. How do you know about that?" He hadn't told her. It was like she was in his head.

And that single thought was all it took to break the connection.

He sighed as he realised he'd just had another 'episode'. At least he'd snapped out of it on his own this time, he supposed.

It did nothing to help him sleep.

CHAPTER FOURTEEN

Chloe had been out walking towards the town limits when she'd first met Zack. She'd just blown off her afternoon classes, annoyed at the shitty grade she'd gotten for a story she'd spent hours working on in her Creative Writing class.

"Fucking pretentious a-hole," she swore, slipping a cigarette out of her shirt cuff and taking her lighter from her rucksack. She lit the cigarette and tossed her bag on the memorial bench by the gate to the walking trail that led out of town and into the woods of Riverton.

After a few puffs, she reached forward and unzipped her bag. Her marked assignment stared back at her. She plucked it from the bag and set the corner on fire with her lighter. It burned slowly. She put the lighter away and watched the paper burn.

"You're not planning on setting the woods on fire, are you?"

The sound of a wry male voice made her jump.

She narrowed her eyes as she dropped the paper. Removing the cigarette from her mouth, she stared the intruder down. He was pale and overdressed for the weather. The coat and gloves were excessive. His eyes were dark, almost same colour as his hair. He was interesting, she decided. He was also new.

"You're not from around here," she told him, flicking ash to the ground.

"Just moved," he said, leaning awkwardly against a tree.

"What year are you in?" She thought of it as a subtle way to ask his age. She wasn't standing around wasting her breath on an under-aged smart-ass.

"I don't go to school," he said, causing her stomach to flip.

He couldn't be too much older than her, but he wasn't at school. It instantly made him seem cooler.

"Yeah? Well, I'm in fifth year," she told him, tossing her cigarette to the ground and stubbing it out with her heel.

"So you're out here burning your homework, then?" He seemed amused. His lips twitched slightly, even if his gaze seemed to catch the ground more often than her eyes.

She shrugged. "What's it to you?"

"Nothing," he said. "I was just bored, and I saw you out here."

She raised an eyebrow. He motioned to the house partially hidden by trees across the road and in the woods.

"You're living in the old murder house?"

"The old what?"

She smiled. "It's just a name. We… the kids around here used to break in on Halloween. It's been abandoned for years."

"So you're telling me I have to wait until Halloween to see you again?"

She looked at him and shook her head. "Not if you let me see inside your house right now."

He cleared his throat, doubt in his eyes for a second. Then he smiled, and her heart skipped a beat.

"Okay," he told her, moving away from the tree he was leaning on.

He was taller than her, even in her heels. She caught his arm as he got closer, holding on as he led the way. She glanced at his gloves again.

"Hey," she said. "Promise me you're not a serial killer."

He seemed to realise what she was getting at. With a small pause, he tugged his gloves off and slipped them into his pocket. "I promise."

She moved her hand down his arm and took his hand. He tensed for a moment, and she wondered what was wrong. "Are you okay?"

He nodded slowly. "Ready for your tour of the murder house?"

"Of course."

She didn't have that moment of doubt she usually experienced before she made a mistake. If he was a psycho, he was hiding it well. She stumbled against him as they walked over the uneven dirt path. He steadied her, stopping her from tripping.

The old house loomed, and from the outside she couldn't tell the difference. It still didn't look lived in. She glanced at him as he opened the door, shifting his sweater sleeve to cover his hand as he turned the handle. "You didn't lock your door?"

He shrugged. "I was two minutes away."

She knew this was the moment her gut instincts should be kicking in telling her this was a bad idea. She was following a stranger into his house in the woods, and she'd left her phone in her bag on the memorial bench.

He walked into the house, and she followed without hesitation. There was a sweet but clinical smell, like bleach covered over with air freshener. The walls were brightly painted. The blue colour of the hallway was a shock. Someone really *was* living in the murder house. She wiped her feet on the mat and walked across the dark carpet to get a closer look at the photo above the phone table.

He cleared his throat again; it seemed to be a nervous habit of his. "I think before you start checking out my stuff, you could at least tell me your name."

She turned. "Does that really matter?"

He seemed speechless. She smiled and moved towards him. He backed into the closed front door.

"Are you afraid of me?"

His dark eyes were wide and entirely focused on her as she pressed up against him.

"You barely know me."

"I know you're harmless," she said, one of her usual lines but that she actually meant, for once, rather than as a taunt. "And you're cute when you're scared."

His heart was pounding hard as she slid a hand around the back of his head, touching his hair. His face flushed as she gazed into his eyes.

"And *you* have a weird way of working your anger out. Not that I don't find it hot. But I'm not looking for anything casual."

She backed away, blinking in surprise. "What?"

He sighed, taking the gloves back out from his pocket.

She watched him put them on, trying to make sense of it.

"So you get to work your anger out and I don't? Not likely, killer."

He gave her a smile that was part grimace. "I'm Zack, by the way."

She rolled her eyes. "Fine. I'm Chloe. Are we all caught up now? Because I could *really* use that work out."

"Can I read it?" He gazed at her levelly.

She frowned. "Read what?"

"The story you were burning out there."

She stared at him. He knew what she'd been doing. For a second, she worried that he might be a vampire with some kind of mind-reading ability. Then logic told her he wasn't. He was human—he'd walked in daylight, and his skin was warm. "How did you know?"

He shrugged. "There's a reason for the gloves."

It all clicked suddenly and drove the last embers of anger from her. She looked him over in wonder. He wasn't a vampire with mind-reading abilities at all. He was a human with those talents. "You're psychic."

"Sort of," he said, shrugging again.

She bit at her lip. "It's probably ashes by now."

"It stopped burning when you dropped it," he told her. "The ground is damp."

"Fine," she said, motioning to the door. "Go get it. I'll wait right here."

He moved hesitantly. "Just, wait *right* there, okay?"

She nodded, curiosity piqued by his words.

The second he left, she pushed at the first door in the hallway. He'd told her to wait right there. He hadn't told her not to peek into the other rooms.

The living room was red and black with a huge TV mounted onto the wall. And the bathroom was sparkling and white. The place was actually a home now. She looked at the picture on the wall; a family portrait. The kid in the middle was young, but he was undoubtedly Zack. He was wearing gloves, even in the photo. She had to smile.

He came back with the slightly scorched story in his gloved hand.

She folded her arms. "What took you so long?"

"This is really good," he said, sounding mildly surprised. "Why did you think his comments were right?"

Her mind drew a blank as she stared at him, not sure how to react. Any guy she'd shown her work to before had been dismissive about it at best. She hadn't expected him to actually read it.

He brushed the paper. "Can I keep this?"

She smiled. "Are you serious?"

"Uh, yeah."

"You can keep it on one condition," she told him. "I get to see your room."

She noticed his mouth had opened and she put on a grin, stopping him with a glance. "Not today, killer. I don't have anything to work out now."

He smiled wryly. "And that would be my fault."

"Try not to look a gift horse in the mouth next time," she advised, walking past him and out of the old murder house.

"Hey," he called after her. "Will you promise to come back sometime?"

She turned. "I promise. Sometime."

***

Chloe awoke sweating at five a.m., tangled in her sheets and breathing heavily. The dream had started off innocuously enough. It had been the day she'd met Zack. The memory had played out exactly as things had happened and then it had turned into a blood-soaked nightmare. She couldn't shake it off as she untangled herself and got up. The floor was cold, but the adrenaline that coursed through her kept her warm.

"I'm not psychic," she whispered, knowing it as the truth but still unable to shake the nightmare.

Zack had been in his house. She'd just left and realised she had to go back. He was exactly the kind of guy she'd been waiting for, and she'd never even known until she'd met him.

She'd run up the steps just as it started to rain. The sound of thunder had followed her as she rushed inside. Zack wasn't where she'd left him. She'd run up the stairs and found him on the landing, his expression slackened by shock. She'd thrown her arms around him and kissed him hard. He'd been too frozen to react. She'd pulled back and caught a blank look in his dark eyes. His face had been spattered with blood. The crimson liquid had stained the walls and his clothes, congealing in a puddle at his bared feet. His hands had been naked and red. A gash in his neck had drawn her attention. She'd gasped as he'd fallen to his knees, clutching at the wound.

That was when she'd woken up in her own warm bed. The image wouldn't leave her.

She threw on her housecoat and rushed to the kitchen, stumbling over her own feet in the dark hallway. The banister saved her from a trip down the stairs, making her wince as she bumped against the wall. She made it to the kettle and sighed in relief.

Switching on the light was her second priority. She did it once the water was boiling. The sight of the pitch-black night through the window made her shiver. She shut the blinds and set about making her mug of tea. The opened notepad on the table drew her attention. She picked up the pen and got to scrawling.

She'd lost the Zack she knew. He'd reset to the guy she'd met at the path to the woods. She shook her head. That wasn't true. The incident had further damaged his already fragile psyche. He'd had some strange episodes ever since it had happened. Not that she knew much about those, only what she'd overheard from eavesdropping on his vampire bodyguard.

She wrote down the things that might make him remember. The story she'd written all those years ago was in one of their bedside cabinets. It was a start.

She tapped the pen off the paper. Her doubts started to kick in. Triggering memories he'd forgotten was something she'd been warned against in the briefing after the incident. There was a lot at stake, not the least of which was Zack's life.

She stared at the page as the kettle boiled. She didn't trust Bridget, never had. The life Zack was living wasn't much of a life anymore. She knew he needed protection, and she knew she could do that by herself.

"We might need to leave town," she murmured as she picked up her tea and put down her pen.

It was something to sleep on. She sighed, knowing her plans would change in the next few hours. She'd be risking her life and his to make him remember. And she didn't even know if he really wanted that. He had to want to remember. Didn't he? Her Zack would have wanted to know. Whatever he'd lost, he was still that guy. Wasn't he?

She sighed, knowing she couldn't risk so much for something so selfish. She put the tea down and snapped the thin pen in her hand, ink staining her fingers. She closed the notebook and went back to bed.

CHAPTER FIFTEEN

Zack spent the morning debating over staying home. The thought of tip-toeing around Bridget and her newly revealed 'feelings' made him groan. But she'd wonder where he was. She'd come over to check on him. At least at the office, he could lock himself away from her.

He got up and got ready. Discovering a new hole in his gloves made him cringe. He'd need them repaired soon or else he'd need a new pair. He put on the sunglasses he'd bought from Chloe's shop before he left the house. He could cope with their boredom better than he could handle the thought of walking around with his eyes unprotected now. Bridget had freaked him out with her tales of what vampires did to psychics they turned. The thought of her fangs biting into her hand made him shiver. She was one of them. Maybe she wasn't like them, but she *was* one of them. He wasn't sure what it meant yet—he only knew he didn't like it.

He posted his lunch order through Cassandra's door as he went past. He saw Chloe going into her store and he smiled. She seemed nice. And she'd been in the arcade a long time; eight years, she'd said. Had he known her before the incident? Blinking, he shook his head. Of course not. What was he thinking? He'd been moved. Witness protection was a serious business. Still, he knew virtually nothing about his past. For the first time since he'd woken up without his memories, it bothered him. Who had he been before?

That was the big question, and it was one he wished he knew the answer to.

***

Bridget had pulled out all the stops with her body-con dress and sultry eye-makeup. She had a plan, and Zack's shy-guy act wasn't going to ruin it. She knew men. They didn't turn down sex, no matter how shy or weird or dull they were. Serve it up hot on a platter and they all chowed down.

She pressed her lips together as Zack entered the office. He avoided meeting her eyes as he dashed into his office. She heard the lock click into place. If he thought that would stop her, he really didn't know what a vampire was.

Rick had been pissed that she'd been forced back to Plan B. She'd assured him that she could handle seduction. He'd laughed and told her he knew she could, but that there was a big difference between controlling a guy's dick and controlling his heart. She'd rolled her eyes at the thought. She wasn't worried about Zack's heart. The shortcut to making a guy crazy for a girl was always through his trousers. She didn't have time to make him fall in love with her, but she knew she could make him think he was. And it was all going to take just one bold move.

She got up, scraping the chair back as she stood. The hardest part had been getting into the right mindset. There was nothing attractive about a broken man. She was an alpha's bitch, one hundred percent. She just had to keep thinking about Kenny. The thought of his touch would get her through one stupid little tryst with the shy psychic.

"Zack," she called through the door, tapping it lightly. "Can we talk?"

"Later," he called out, not bothering to follow up with an excuse.

She picked the lock with a hairpin. Getting inside, she smiled at the look of shock on the guy's pale face. "We need to talk, Zack."

"Um, I'm busy…" he tried, shuffling papers on his desk.

"There's something that's been killing me. I had to tell you. I know it's no good for your condition, but I'm sick of pretending you mean nothing to me." She locked the door behind her and moved around to block his escape. "I'm not just a bodyguard, Zack."

She unzipped her dress and wriggled out of it. Naked underneath, she stood before him. "Please, tell me you remember? It's been so long since we made love."

Zack's jaw dropped. He spun in his chair.

"Shit, the vampire's being sexy! Steve, tell me what to do."

"Did you take your pills, Zack? It doesn't sound like you've been taking your pills."

"I don't want her anywhere near me. I don't know what to do."

Bridget sighed.

"Enough of this shit," she muttered, moving around to face Zack during his 'therapy session'. She smiled tightly. "Fuck the vampire, Zack. *That's* what you need to do."

Zack blinked slowly, his frown telling her he was coming back to himself. His dark eyes met hers when he snapped back into focus.

"We can't do this, Bridget."

She tried to move, to slide her fangs into place with the intention of biting into his thigh through his trouser leg. Chloe's commands stopped her. She couldn't hurt him no matter how badly she wanted to. So she was screwed if she couldn't get Zack to fall for her. She tried a sweet smile instead. "Why not?"

"I don't… I don't like you like that." He shrugged apologetically.

She backed off quickly, throwing her dress back on and leaving the room. She couldn't even force fake tears to guilt him into at least a show of sympathy. Her irritation was too close to the surface. This was mission impossible, and she only had one more day to pull it off. She sat at her desk, straightening her clothes and trying to think.

"Shit," she cursed, tapping her nails off the desk as she tried to come up with her next plot. She couldn't turn Zack herself. Chloe had closed down that option. She needed another way. Another vampire. A smile started to form on her face. Chloe hadn't told her not to bite anyone else…

***

Chloe attempted to check her stock to place a new order to her supplier. Every time she started to count, her mind drifted. Maybe it was time to start planning a new life. The old one was gone. She should use it as a chance to start over. Move away or plan an extended trip to someplace exciting, exotic.

None of her ideas sparked any semblance of passion. She sighed and tried to keep her head on her job.

Amira came hopping into the shop at lunchtime, a latte in one hand and a tea in the other. She placed the tea on Chloe's counter and grinned, her whole face lighting up. "Hey."

"Hey," Chloe said with a smile. "How's—"

"Larry keeps asking me out," she blurted. She waved her phone under Chloe's nose. "I don't know what to do."

Chloe took a breath. She should have known this would come up. Larry had only been the object of Amira's infatuation a few crushes ago. She'd hoped he was out of her system now, but it really didn't look like it. "I thought you liked that guy from class?"

She screwed up her face. "He had like, three other girls lined up on Tinder. I checked his phone on our date."

"Well, then…" She wasn't sure what to say. Larry was a good guy, but he was also a creature of the night now. Amira had no idea those things existed, let alone how to protect herself against them.

"I know he has bad skin, but he's cute, right?" Amira's hopeful eyes met hers and she broke. "And I did have that crush on him like, all of last summer. He got all flustered when I told him he looked good at that night out, remember?"

She was gushing on, and Chloe knew she'd have to say something to get her to stop.

"He's a sweet guy. He's… a little bit older than you, though. Are you sure about why he's asking you out?"

Chloe wasn't so sure she wanted to encourage her. As much as she liked them both, she didn't want Amira to get hurt. Larry hadn't seen how his improved body was going to affect women yet. And he didn't have control of his thirst. That would take time.

"Are you saying he's only after me for my hot body?" Amira raised an eyebrow. "He's only two years older. That's my minimum dating age for a guy, anyway. I'm not sure what my maximum is, but maybe I won't need to worry about that if things work out with Larry."

Chloe cringed. She couldn't imagine Amira being okay with a boyfriend who would stay young and sexy while she aged. Never mind one who could kill her by accident if he wasn't being careful. She tried to think of something negative to say that might get through. There was nothing that wouldn't be a blatant lie, and Chloe wasn't great at making those sound believable.

She sighed. "Just don't go rushing into anything, okay?"

Amira snorted.

"It's just a night out. I wonder what I'm going to wear." She sipped on her hot drink and gazed out of the shop window.

Chloe wondered what Larry had told her. She'd already

told him he needed to stay in for the next few weeks. Apparently, he wasn't listening to her advice. She wasn't all that surprised. She'd just have to make him listen before he went out on his 'date'.

She chatted to the girl for twenty minutes until Amira had to get back to work. A couple of high school girls browsed after that, eventually buying matching skull charm bracelets. She smiled as she rung them up. The rest of the day passed without too much dwelling. She didn't even think about Zack until she bumped into him outside the arcade.

***

Zack shuddered as he left the office. He wasn't going in to work the next day. Bridget was acting insane, and he didn't want to witness another clothes-shedding incident. It was too messed up.

He left the arcade and sighed at the onslaught of rain. The sky was overcast and miserable. Hesitating to step out into it, he was nudged forward as someone else came out of the arcade.

"Oh, hey," Chloe said, sounding surprised.

"Hi," he said, looking her outfit over and thinking about offering her his coat. The short skirt and thin sweater didn't look very warm.

She put up an umbrella. "Will this rain never end?" She looked at him. "You want under?"

He smiled. "We might be going in different directions."

"I live close to where you do," she said, shrugging.

He nodded and took the umbrella. She took his arm as they walked, keeping close and under shelter from the rain. It wasn't a typical woman's umbrella but a golf umbrella. He wondered if it was hers.

"You can have my coat," he offered, wishing he'd said it before she'd put the umbrella up.

She smiled. "I don't mind the cold. It's kind of refreshing."

He didn't mind it for different reasons. He liked having her close, clinging to him like she needed him. "This is going to seem like a weird question…"

She stopped walking, and he looked at her. Making eye contact was going to make it even weirder. What was he doing? He shouldn't even be thinking about asking. He took a breath, determined to get it out.

"Did we know each other, before? I don't remember anything. I just… I'm really starting to wish I did."

She looked away, biting at her lip. When she looked back, she sighed softly. "It's dangerous for you to remember anything, Zack. It might be better if you don't ask those kinds of questions."

He nodded slowly. She was probably right. They walked on in silence, just a few more feet when she stopped walking again. His hopes lit up until he realised she wasn't stopping to answer his question or elaborate on what she'd already said.

She moved back, letting go of his arm. "This is my stop."

He looked at the house, wishing it rang some sort of bells for him. Wishing something did—anything. Even if it meant he had to remember Bridget had been his girlfriend. He didn't care if it meant he would remember who he'd been. "Your umbrella…"

Chloe turned and shook her head. "Keep it."

***

Chloe got inside and closed the door, her heart pounding. She was already kicking herself for the answer she'd given to Zack's question. She'd wanted to know if he felt like that, if he wanted to remember. Well, apparently, he did, and what did she do with that?

"Damn it," she snapped. It had happened. She'd had her moment. It had passed quickly, and all she'd done was remind Zack that it was dangerous to think about wanting to remember his past.

CHAPTER SIXTEEN

The cloudy sky fit Bridget's mood as she walked home, her clingy dress soaked through by the time she got to her flat. She tore it off in a fury. Men didn't turn her down, they never could.

He's not a man, she reminded herself. He was barely even functioning as a human.

After drying off, she put on an even sexier dress and worked at calming herself down. Her cats tried to help, mewling mournfully around her legs as she moved towards the living room. She picked up Genevieve, but stroking her soft fur didn't de-stress Bridget the way it usually would.

Her gaze fell to Arthur through the kitchen doorway. The king cat was steering well clear of her mood. He sat on top of the fridge, eyes almost closed. As if he could tell she wasn't going to be calmed by anything less than brutality.

She sat down in her usual arm chair, the cat curling into her lap. Petting the animal made it purr. Her stroking became harder as she let her rage out. The cat's ears went up, but it couldn't move. Bridget's nails dug into Genevieve's skin, causing the cat to yelp. Her claws shot out, and Bridget's anger climaxed. She took hold of the animal and twisted its goddamned stupid body. The spine snapped with a crack that relaxed her shoulders. Claws were still embedded in her leg and thigh. She yanked the dead cat upwards and threw it across the room. The bloodied spots on her bared leg were nothing. They healed quickly and she wiped up the blood, sucking it off her fingers as Genevieve's brothers hissed at her.

"You want to play, little boys?" She narrowed her eyes. "Just try me. I dare you."

She kicked at Lancelot as she walked past the creatures. What good were they if they couldn't even cheer her up? She scowled at Arthur as she opened the fridge. He regarded her blankly, closing his eyes. She looked at the bags of blood inside. It was an insult that she had to drink animal blood. She smiled to herself as she made her decision and closed the fridge. She was eating out tonight.

***

Larry buttoned his shirt, chewing on his lower lip. If Chloe came around, she was going to mess up his plans again. He knew it. And this time, his plans were looking too good to be true. Amira had agreed to meet him at a pub. She'd even put a kiss on her reply.

He took a breath, realised he really hadn't needed to, and shrugged that thought off before he could think about it too much. He cleared his throat and called Chloe.

"Come on," he muttered, pacing the hall as he waited for her to pick up.

"Larry, hey," Chloe said.

She sounded distracted or pissed off, he wasn't sure which.

"Um, hey, so…"

"You asked Amira out." She sounded mad.

"Uh," he said, wondering how she'd found out. He cringed. "You caught me. We're just meeting for a drink. I've not even had any blood, I promise."

She sighed. "Go and drink two pints before you go out."

"Eh, I… what?"

"You can't go out unless you're full. If you get hungry, you could bite someone."

"So I'm allowed out, then?"

"On two conditions."

He punched the air. "Awesome."

"First one, and do it while I'm on the phone," she said, pausing. "Go drink those two pints of blood right now."

He obeyed her command, not even caring if he was doing it because she was ordering him around or because he actually wanted to. He'd waited a long time for a girl like Amira to give him a chance. He'd do whatever Chloe told him to do right now, which was just as well considering she wanted him to do something else, too.

He sucked down the blood, sighing in satisfaction when he finished. He wiped at his mouth and looked out of the kitchen window. Rain was pelting the glass in big blobs. The weather was shit, but he couldn't get rid of the grin that had appeared on his face.

"And the other thing?" he asked.

"Right. Listen up, Larry, because this is important. You will not bite anyone tonight. You will go for a drink with Amira, and you will make sure she gets home safe at the end of the night." She muttered something before she spoke again. "You can't drink anything when you're out. You'll have to pretend to drink."

He nodded while she spoke. Her commanding voice was different from her usual conversational tone. She'd commanded him not to bite anyone. She was only giving him advice now.

"Um, why am I not drinking anything?" He was going to a pub. Not drinking would be kind of hard.

"You're a vampire now, Larry. They don't eat or drink anything but blood."

"Oh." That kind of sucked.

"Yeah. So, anyway… call me if you need anything."

He agreed and hung up. This was it. He rushed into the bathroom to finish getting ready. It was probably an idea to brush his teeth considering he'd just been drinking blood.

***

Zack stood outside Chloe's house for a while, not quite sure what he was thinking. She hadn't answered his question. She hadn't told him if they'd known each other before. He wasn't sure what he thought that meant, but it made him want to go and knock on her door.

He stood there in the rain, staring at her door for ages until he realised how creepy it would seem to her if she saw he was still out there. He walked away, deciding that returning the umbrella would at least give him another chance to speak to her.

She knew something. Whatever it was, it was important. He'd seen it in her face.

***

Chloe put down the phone and resisted the urge to open the blinds wider. Zack hadn't left, and her heart pounded as she waited to see what he would do. Hope burned through her as she realised her answer hadn't satisfied him.

"Thank God," she whispered, unable to move from the window until he started to walk away.

She moved to the other window to watch him go, staying hidden by refusing to switch the lights on. He paused and looked back at the house before he picked up his pace.

Sighing, she collapsed onto her overstuffed couch. He wanted to remember who he was. She was sure of that now. A million and one ideas whipped through her head, most of them selfish. He hadn't known who she was when she'd rushed to the hospital after his attack, and he didn't know who she was now. She had to accept that.

What could she do to help him? She folded her arms, staring up at the ceiling. Answering his questions would be a start. She could avoid anything about her and him. She didn't want him to look at her as if she was crazy. The way he'd looked when she'd seen him in that hospital bed. Tears had streamed down her face. He hadn't understood, and the bemused smile after she'd kissed him had been too much to take. Apparently, he'd forgotten that encounter, too. The doctors had told her he was out of it at that point. It wasn't until the Council reports came through that she was told he needed to be treated a certain way. It was going to be dangerous for him to remember anything. No one was to remind him of his old life. They couldn't take him out of town. Transporting him would only risk an abduction.

She closed her eyes. Their first kiss flooded back to her. It had been a rainy day three months after they'd met. He'd been trying his hardest to ask her out, and she'd been teasing him about it. As much as she liked spending time with him, she was starting to worry that he might be kind of creepy. Her friends had been worried about her spending so much time with some weird older guy. She'd overheard them talking about it. She'd wanted to storm into the room and defend Zack, but she'd hesitated, wondering if they were right.

That was the day she'd realised she didn't care what her friends thought. Zack was always there when she needed him. He didn't make any moves, and he wasn't trying to rush her into bed like a lot of older guys in the same situation would.

"Hey, what's up?" He'd met her at their usual spot by the bench.

She'd gone out there to tell him she couldn't see him anymore, but the second she'd seen his face, she'd known that plan wasn't going to work. She'd ditched her bag on the bench.

"When you touch me, what is it that you see?"

"See?" He'd looked as if he didn't get what she was

asking. He'd been wearing his gloves, as usual. He'd only taken them off when she'd wanted to hold hands.

"Psychics see things, right?"

"Well…" he'd trailed off, gazing out towards his house.

She'd been half-afraid he'd know she'd doubted him or her feelings for him.

The overcast sky had been threatening to pour all day. It had started to drizzle, but she'd barely felt it as she'd watched his expression change.

"It's kind of complicated," he'd said, finally, with a cute little smile that didn't quite let him get away with the lack of an answer.

"Like the first time I held your hand, you knew what had happened with that story and my idiot teacher."

He'd nodded slowly.

"I get flashes," he'd admitted. "Not all the time. You were new to me, and your emotions were running high. That's what triggered the flash."

She'd taken it in. "So what would happen if we kissed?"

He'd shaken his head. "I honestly don't know."

"Have you never kissed someone before?" She'd find that hard to believe. He might've been shy and odd, but he was still a good-looking guy.

"It's different now," he'd said. "My abilities have fully developed."

"So you don't know." She hadn't been sure what to do. If he found out she'd doubted him, would he push her away? She really didn't think she wanted that. She'd bitten her lip until her mind decided *what the hell?* "My friends think you're weird. I wasn't sure if I thought the same."

He'd given her a bemused smile. "Well, I do live in the woods and wear gloves to keep myself sane."

She'd laughed. "You also haven't tried anything with me. And I've been putting out some pretty heavy take-me vibes."

"That doesn't mean I'm not interested," he'd told her. "I just… I don't want to push it."

"Push what?" She'd taken a step closer, wondering how he'd react if she threw her arms around his neck. She hadn't been quite ready to find out.

"My luck," he'd said, gazing at her. "I'm weird, and you're smart and pretty enough to find a less strange guy to hang around with."

"Maybe I don't want a less strange guy. Maybe I want to hang around with you," she'd said.

He'd taken a slow breath and removed his gloves. She'd seen them drop to the ground before he'd cupped her face in his hands and kissed her. The rain had started to hit harder as she'd kissed back, arms around his neck, pushing on to her toes against him. His hands hadn't moved from her head. His thumbs had stroked her cheeks before his hands had moved through her hair. His kiss had been achingly slow and soft. She could barely think straight by the time he'd slipped his tongue into her mouth. Vaguely aware of the rumbling sky above them, she'd pressed close against him and grasped at the back of his head as the drops of water had started to pelt them and soak their clothes. She'd been gasping when he'd moved back, her lips tender and her body shivering.

"So," she'd said. "Did you see anything?"

His dark eyes had burned into hers as he'd smiled. "I didn't see anything, but I definitely felt something."

"Me, too," she'd said, moving back in a mild daze as he'd taken off his coat.

He'd wrapped it around her shoulders, warming her. She'd barely noticed him picking up his gloves.

"I should probably walk you home," he'd said, grabbing her bag from the bench.

She'd smiled, thinking about her friends across the street seeing him walk her to her front door. "What's the rush?"

He'd laughed. "It's pissing down."

"Maybe I want to watch that shirt go see-through," she'd told him.

"I'm sure you'll have other chances to see that," he'd said, taking her hand.

He'd slipped the gloves into his pocket. It had made her smile. He didn't like to take them off, but for her, he had.

CHAPTER SEVENTEEN

Larry's nerves kicked in as he got out of the car and rushed towards the doors to the pub. He'd called a taxi to avoid getting soaked on the way there. Putting on a coat would have hidden his new muscular body from sight. He'd felt pretty confident until he walked up to the glass doors of the pub.

Now, he wasn't sure how he'd make it through the date without downing several shots at a bare minimum. Not being able to drink was going to make things awkward. Amira had told him she'd meet him inside.

He paused and checked his new and improved reflection in the glass panes of the door. His smile returned, albeit less brightly, and he pushed the door inwards, entering the bar.

The smells, sights, and sounds drowned him as he stepped into the brightly lit room. He squinted as he waited for his senses to calm. Everything was too loud, too bright. Chloe hadn't warned him that his senses would be so easily stimulated. Maybe she didn't know. She wasn't actually a vampire, after all. It was a good job he'd already sort of worked it out when he'd gone to watch TV at home. He couldn't sit as close to the screen anymore. And he didn't like it too loud.

He stuffed his hands into his pockets. He'd almost forgotten to hit the cash-line. One look at his bank account and he knew he was going to need a new job, and soon.

"Larry?"

Amira's honey-sweet voice was instantly recognisable.

He turned and saw her looking absolutely stunning in a cream knee-length dress. Her hair was loosely curled and hung to her shoulders. Her dark eyes widened as she looked him over.

"Antibiotics," he blurted. "I had a throat infection. Turns out antibiotics are like Clearasil on crack."

She pressed her lips together. "Right. So, how come it took you so long to ask me out?"

He opened his mouth and closed it again. Had he heard her right?

"I mean, we talk like, almost every day at work," she went on. "And you ask other girls out."

Crap, she was seriously asking. He swallowed. "I…um…"

"Relax. I'm teasing," she said with a smile. "Go buy me a drink."

"What kind?"

"What do I usually drink?"

He could remember what she drank from work nights out. He hadn't hit on her at those, either, just Chloe and Cassandra, and the woman from Rico's clothes store he could never quite remember the name of. He'd always avoided asking Amira out. A knock-back from any of the others, he could laugh off. He was a kid to them, a joke. He had no chance. But her? Some small part of him had been holding out for her, hoping for some kind of sign, and now his chance was here.

He nodded as he moved towards the bar, trying to keep himself from making an ass of himself. He ordered a white wine spritzer for her and a vodka for himself. He'd already decided vodka would be the easiest thing to pretend-drink. It was clear liquid. He could spill drops whenever her head was turned, and she'd never know.

She waved from a booth she'd scored while he was at the bar. He got in beside her, and the proximity let him smell the peach shampoo she always used as if her hair was right up against his face.

"Are you okay, Larry?"

"I'm great," he said, realising it was true as he put the drinks down. "I didn't ask you out before because I thought you could do better."

She winced and he wondered when he'd stop shooting himself in the foot. Sudden good looks didn't prevent verbal diarrhoea, apparently.

"Would you please relax?" She shook her head. "This is supposed to be a date. We should be having fun."

She was right. He had to calm down. He picked up the vodka and drained the glass. Dutch courage. Or not. As he swallowed, he remembered he wasn't supposed to. What would happen? Dread coursed through him. He wondered how well Amira would take it if he dashed off to call Chloe right now.

"O-Kay. So when are you coming back to work?"

He smiled wryly.

"I might be done with the security guard gig," he told her.

She raised an eyebrow. "You got another job?"

"I… might be joining the police."

"Well, you would look good in the uniform," she told him, her gaze drifting to his arm. "What have you been up to these last few days? Were you just popping antibiotics and working out all day?"

Her hand ran over his shirt sleeve, and he held back the urge to lean in and kiss her. As good as she looked and smelled, he didn't want to do something stupid and put her off him now.

"I work out most days. Lately, I mean," he said, wishing it didn't sound like bullshit.

His sudden muscles and cleared up skin had seemed like good things up until now. He hadn't thought much about how he'd explain them. The only good thing he had left was that Amira had agreed to the date without knowing how his looks had changed. She'd liked him before this had happened. Knowing that made him smile.

"You were always good enough for me, Larry," she told him, her gaze on his when he looked up.

"I didn't think so," he said. "You date smart guys. I barely even passed my standard grades."

"That was why you never asked me out before?"

He shrugged, wishing he'd gotten more vodka. Clearly, Chloe didn't know what she was talking about when it came to vampires and booze. "I always wanted to."

She reached out and touched his face. Her soft fingers felt so warm and good against his skin. He could smell the vanilla perfume she was wearing, and he could hear the pulsing of her blood. The vein in her wrist was so close to his mouth. The urge to bite came and went. Chloe's order working on him, he supposed. Amira pulled his head down towards hers.

"Kiss me," she said, stopping just short of initiating it herself.

He lowered his lips to hers, closing his eyes when they met. He let her take the lead, afraid to make the mistakes he'd made with Chloe. She pulled him closer and he deepened the kiss, the sweet taste of her mouth driving his senses wild. It was everything he'd hoped it would be. He never wanted it to end. She put on the brakes after a few minutes, breathing heavily as she gazed at him, her lips swollen.

"Okay, good," she said with a grin. "I just wanted to check the chemistry. It's definitely there."

He smiled. "Maybe we should check again, just in case."

She pushed him back into his seat.

He couldn't wipe the grin from his face as she picked up her drink.

***

Bridget smiled as she walked into the bar. Her sense of smell had picked up something tastier than a willing victim. A baby vampire was in the building. A vampire without a clan. Her smile widened.

"Hey, gorgeous." A guy with a cocky smile and whiskey breath blocked her path.

Her smile turned to ice as she stared him down. "Get out of my way."

He was human, and he could have been useful before she'd had a change of plans. As it was, he was nothing more than a cockroach to step on. She gave him a shove and moved past him.

"What the… Slag!" he shouted after her.

She didn't waste her time responding. The new vampire was lurking in a dark corner with a pretty human girl. The girl from the slightly less trashy clothes store in the arcade. She sucked in a breath as she took in the identity of the vampire. The greasy-haired teenage security guard! She scowled, one hand dropping to her hip. What were the chances? Pretty high, she realised as she remembered where she'd come across the damned Winter clan vampire in the first place.

It really didn't matter who he was. She had a job to do and not much time left to do it.

With her sweetest smile, she approached the cutesy couple in their secluded booth.

"Hey, gorgeous," she greeted Larry, her gaze devoted to him.

He swallowed as he stared back. "Hey…"

"Get lost, cougar," Amira snapped, putting her drink down.

Bridget ignored the girl. Her compulsion would force Larry to follow her. She would use him to turn Zack. "Get up, Larry. You're coming with me."

He shifted with a wince. "I'm coming with you."

"Larry!" Amira yanked his arm and he fell back on his ass. "What are you…"

Bridget forced a smile and turned to the girl. "Be quiet and sit still."

Agape, Amira did as told. Bridget concentrated on Larry, getting him out of the booth and away from his possessive girlfriend.

"Amira, I…" He turned his head, and Bridget sighed.

She pulled his head around to face her. "You will shut up and follow me. Now."

He did as told, but Bridget bit her lip when the scent of the girl caught up to her. She hadn't eaten yet, and Zack would need to be fed once he was turned. She turned and told Amira to get up and follow them, too. Forcing Larry to watch his girlfriend get drained would be good training for him. He could be an asset to her clan, not as much as Zack would be, but still… he could have his uses.

CHAPTER EIGHTEEN

Zack put the umbrella in his bathtub and moved around the flat, taking his coat and sunglasses off. The conversation with Chloe was still bothering him. He almost wanted to go right back to her house with the umbrella just to get the chance to speak to her again. She knew something, and she wanted to tell him. He'd analysed her reaction to death. She definitely wanted to tell him, and whatever it was, it would be better than the nothing he had now.

His doorbell rang just as he went to get the umbrella. He kept it in his gloved hand as he went to answer the door. Checking through the peephole, he saw it was just his neighbour, Kenny.

"Oh, hi," he said, opening the door.

"Everything okay?"

"Um…"

"You were stomping around." The guy sounded suspicious.

"I didn't think I was. Sorry," Zack said, wondering what was up with the guy.

"Going somewhere?"

He had noticed the umbrella in Zack's hand. Oh, right, he was a cop, and he was supposed to be nosy about his comings and goings.

"No. Just…tidying up."

"Oh. Well. Let me know if you speak to Bridget."

"Bridget?" Zack's curiosity rose.

"I need to speak to her." The guy didn't elaborate. He just moved swiftly down the hall.

Zack closed, locked, and bolted his door. He put the umbrella down and decided he needed a cup of tea. Maybe the rain would go off and he could return the umbrella without looking like an idiot.

***

Kenny called Bridget again, got no answer, and threw the phone across the room. What good was a girlfriend who wasn't there when he needed her? He shook his head.

"Fucking stupid bitch," he cursed.

This was all her fault. The Council was putting him on probation, which basically meant he'd be working without pay and subject to random checks. He was suspected of manipulating his abilities, which could only mean one thing. Bridget had reported him for ordering her around. As if she didn't get off on it. He always let her go when she told him to stop. She always smiled when she realised he'd commanded her to do something she liked doing anyway.

He got her, and she got him. It was what made them work. He wasn't a very romantic kind of guy, but he'd do almost anything for Bridget, and he'd done some things already that he knew could have gotten him into trouble with the Council. He hadn't cared because those things had been for her. But now? She'd better have a damn good explanation for this.

***

Bridget led Larry and his bitchy girlfriend to Zack's flat. She got her key out once they were on the stairwell. She'd had enough questions from Amira when they'd left the bar, so she'd compelled the girl to shut up. Now they were good little children, following her to their fates. She smiled. The day was finally looking up.

Getting to Zack's door, she stopped and listened intently. The sound of the TV was faint. He was in the living room, then. She moved forward with her keys, and a noise from her right made her turn.

"Kenny," she said. "You nearly gave me a heart attack."

He was pissed. She'd seen that look before, usually right after a call from his Council.

"Get in here," he told her, folding his arms.

She moved forward, cursing internally. He always had to throw his weight around at the worst of times. She moved involuntarily and her anger grew with every step. Her bespelled followers moved with her.

"What is it, Kenny? I'm busy right now."

"Screw that. You owe me an explanation."

Whatever was going on, he wasn't going to be consoled without speaking to her. She turned her head. "Larry, Amira.

Go to Zack's door and visit with him. Wait there for me. Do not leave."

She kept walking until she was in Kenny's flat, only looking back when Larry and Amira were at Zack's door. She sighed and turned her glower on Kenny.

"This had better be good."

"Funny, I was about to say the same thing to you."

***

Zack got up cautiously. The knocking on the door was eerily light. He didn't think it was Kenny again, and it certainly wasn't Bridget. He checked through the peep-hole and saw two familiar faces from the arcade. Surprised, he opened the door.

"Uh, hi," he said.

"Zack, we came to visit," Amira said, sounding oddly flat.

"Yeah. And Bridget's going to be here soon, too," Larry put in with an equal amount of enthusiasm.

"Em, okay, I guess. Come in," he said, letting them in.

Did everyone at work know where he lived? He shrugged the thought off as he locked the door behind them. "Tea or coffee?"

Amira shrugged. "We were on a date."

He glanced at Larry, who nodded.

"We were." He shrugged as well and then Amira took his hand.

"So… no tea or coffee."

Zack moved on to the living room. He hit standby on

the TV remote, not wanting them to notice the trashy sitcom he'd gotten caught up watching. His brain was easily amused these days. It was sort of embarrassing.

"Larry got really hot," Amira said, sitting down on the couch. She still had a weirdly flat tone to her voice.

"Amira fancied me before, anyway," Larry said.

Zack started to wonder what was going on, more so when the two of them started to make-out on his couch.

"What the hell…" He got up and went into the kitchen, dialling Bridget's number. Those two had to be on drugs or on Aftershocks at a bare minimum.

He sighed. Her phone was ringing out. He tapped his fingers on the counter top and considered Chloe's number. She knew them both, at least. Maybe she could help.

***

Bridget listened to Kenny rant, and all she could think about was how much better he'd look with his top off. When he finished and waited expectantly for her to speak, she let her mind check over the insane accusations he'd flung at her.

"Kenny, sweetheart, why would I want you on probation? The last thing I need is the Council poking their noses into my business. They don't need to know about us." She shook her head. "If anyone has it in for you, it's that little bitch Chloe and her stuck-up, goody-two-shoes attitude."

He was drinking in her every word. She almost wished she was lying to him. It would have been a thrill to get away with it.

He grabbed her suddenly and kissed her hard. She kissed back, and he pressed against her. She knew she wasn't getting out of his flat without pleasuring him, but she also knew exactly how to turn him on and finish him off faster than he could jerk himself off. So she did her dutiful girlfriend part and turned to leave.

He caught her hand. "I could make you stick around."

"You could. But you don't have to. I'll be back. I've got things to do, but when they're done…" She held her breath that he'd let her go without a fight.

His sated state seemed to mellow him slightly. He let her go.

She kissed his cheek and dashed out of the flat. It was time, finally, for Plan C.

***

Chloe answered the phone before she could think twice about it. Zack was actually calling her?

"Hello?"

"Chloe?"

"It's me. What's up?" She tried to keep her voice steady.

"I, um, well… it's kind of weird, and I didn't know who to call." He sounded so awkward.

She smiled. "What's going on?"

"A couple of people who work in the arcade came to visit. I'm not sure why, but supposedly Bridget's coming over, too. Only she hasn't yet, and now I think they're dry humping on my couch," he told her, stage-whispering the last part.

Chloe was stuck between amusement and horror. "Who's there, Zack?"

"The security guard and the Indian girl from the clothes shop."

He clearly couldn't remember their names. For some reason, it drew a wry smile out of Chloe. Until she remembered the security guard was Larry, who was now a vampire. Her smile froze.

"I'll be right over." She hung up, grabbed her keys, shoved on her boots, and left.

***

Zack jumped up at the knock. He rushed to the door, thinking it was fast for Chloe.

Checking the peephole, he took in Bridget's irritable expression and hesitated. Something was weird about the whole situation. He shook it off. Bridget's job was to protect him. He knew he could trust her. Audrey had told him not to, but she wasn't real so her opinions shouldn't count. He opened the door and let Bridget in.

"What's going on?" He kept his voice low.

She closed the door behind her and moved towards the living room. "It's happening. We need to move quickly."

His brain rushed to keep up with her words. "It's happening? What…"

She pushed the living room door open, made a noise of disgust, and strode forward.

"Cut that out," she snapped, capturing the attention of the young lovers on his couch immediately. They both turned to her, falling away from each other.

Zack hesitated at the doorway. He didn't like the way the kids' faces slackened when Bridget spoke. There was something hideously eerie about it.

"Separate," she said as the girl straightened her dress and the guy folded his arms. She turned to Zack, shaking her head. "They've been drinking, if you couldn't tell."

He tried a smile, but it didn't want to surface. Swallowing, he tugged at his hair. "So, it's happening?"

What was happening? The vampires were there? He was too freaked out to ask. He didn't want to contemplate what it all meant. Where the hell were his sunglasses?

She nodded, glancing back. "Larry, get over here."

The tall guy got to his feet and moved towards her.

"How are you doing that?" Zack flushed when he realised he'd said it out loud.

"I'm a vampire, Zack. It's one of my many talents." Her irises seemed to flash red for a second. He blinked and they were back to normal. She sighed softly. "Amira, restrain Zack for me."

The girl got up as Zack realised what was happening. He stumbled backwards, and Amira rushed at him, slamming him into the wall in the hallway. He groaned at the pain his shoulder took as the girl's hand knocked it into the wall. She remained holding him there, determination in her gaze.

He pushed against her, and Bridget snorted.

"The girl works out, Zack. You're too soft. Give it up." She turned to the guy. "Larry, fangs."

His mouth opened, his teeth sharpening in an instant.

He looked to Bridget, and she smiled.

"Get over here and rip Zack's throat out."

***

Pushing at the girl, Zack gasped in a breath.

"This is it, Steve. I'm dying."

"Don't be so melodramatic. Nothing's wrong. Calm down."

"I'm about to have my throat ripped out by a vampire. I don't think that's melodramatic!"

"Have you been taking your pills, Zack?"

"What? No. Who cares? I'm about to be murdered!"

***

The hand that caught Larry by the throat was strong and familiar. Bridget's enjoyment muted itself as she turned to find her lover standing in her way. He had a look of betrayal on his handsome face. She smirked as Larry's jaw moved, his teeth snapping inches from Zack's spaced-out face.

"What is this?" Kenny sounded furious.

"This is Plan C, Kenny." She knew he couldn't control two vampires at once, but she wasn't going to have very long to convince him that she was doing what was best for everyone. "Your Council is abandoning you. Why don't you come with me? I'll be leaving as soon as—"

"As soon as what, Bridget?"

Chloe's irate voice hit her ears, and her gaze moved past her lover. The punky girl was standing just inside the front door, a stake in one hand.

Bridget rolled her eyes. "Piss off, Chloe."

"Let me past," Chloe demanded, fortunately directing her command at Kenny.

Kenny was still holding onto Larry. Amira still had Zack restrained, though from his babbling, it was obvious he wasn't in the room with them right now. This could still go Bridget's way. She looked at Kenny, meeting his own angry stare and reflecting it back at him.

"How can you just stand there while that bitch acts all high and mighty? Aren't you going to rip into her for what she did to you?"

Kenny turned his head slightly and looked back at Bridget.

"What have you got left to lose, Kenny?"

She knew she'd hit a nerve when he closed his eyes. In that brief moment, she knew he was making his choice. His grip slackened, and Larry yanked himself free.

"You fucking…" Chloe's impending insult was killed by Kenny's backhand punch. She crashed to the ground, dropping the stake.

Bridget smiled as Larry bit into Zack's throat. Her trepidation vanished as she saw her plan unfold. Her intent was to turn Zack, not to 'hurt' him. She hadn't been sure the distinction would matter until Larry followed her orders.

"Finally." She looked at Kenny as he moved closer to watch. "We've got him."

***

Chloe jumped to her feet, unable to see the stake. Kenny was blocking her path, but she had to stop what was happening and she knew what her best bet was. She glanced around and picked up the golf umbrella she'd given Zack. She could see the blank stare on his face as Larry drank from him.

Please, please, let him be okay.

Tearing her gaze away, she moved quickly. Kenny's arm blocked her first strike but she got in a second well-placed thrust before he turned on her. Bridget fell to her knees, staring at the end of the umbrella sticking out of her chest before she burst into ashes. Larry fell away from Zack, dazed and blood-spattered, followed by Amira who snapped back into focus and shrieked at the blood on her arms. Bridget's control broke the second she died.

Kenny turned to Chloe, rage in his gaze, and she shrugged at him, breathing hard from the exertion and shock of what she'd done. It wasn't her place to kill vampires. She'd never done anything like that before. She trembled as she looked at the ash-covered umbrella on the carpet.

"You're going to pay for that." Kenny's fists were balled as he advanced on her, venom in his tone.

She glanced at Zack as he slid down the wall. He looked dead—glassy-eyed and covered in blood.

Hot tears pricked her eyes. If she failed him after all this, she didn't know what she'd do.

Kenny's first punch connected hard, followed by another as he roared at her. The air was knocked from her lungs as she was thrown onto her back.

Her vision blurred as Larry attacked Kenny from behind. He was no match for the older, bulkier guy. Even if he wasn't a necromancer, Larry didn't stand a chance.

"Back the fuck off, dead-boy."

The single command had Larry back off and stand stock-still while Kenny advanced on her again, cursing and spitting his fury out as he got ready to kill her.

He fell on her, his hands gripping her neck. She could see the blind hatred in his eyes as he started to choke her. Her hands scratched at his wrists as she tried to make him let go.

She couldn't force in a breath. She knew this was it—she was going to die. Closing her eyes, she stopped trying to fight it. That was when his grip slackened. What the...?

He fell on top of her like a lead weight. She pushed hard to get him off and rolled out from under his heft, aching all over as she moved. She didn't take her gaze from him, and he didn't move as she gasped in a few panicked breaths, trying to stop the shaking that her limbs were doing. He was out cold, blood trickling through his blond hair to his forehead. She looked up and saw Amira standing over her, half a vase in her hand and shock in her big, dark eyes.

"Call an ambulance," Chloe said, her voice strained and quiet.

Amira was quick to glance around and grab the phone. Her voice sounded far away as Chloe moved towards Zack, pulling herself across the floor, too weakened to trust her legs to carry her. He was breathing shallowly. She looked at Larry helplessly standing frozen in place, a look of horror in his eyes and blood staining his mouth.

She cleared her throat to command the vampire. "Larry, come over here and heal Zack's wound."

Her voice was still a reedy whisper, but the vampire did as he was told. She breathed a relieved sigh and rested her shoulder against the wall, taking one of Zack's limp hands in her own. He started to whisper quietly, and she leaned in closer to hear him as Larry finished his job and backed away.

***

"I don't know why you're still speaking to me, Audrey. I know you're not real."

His big sister sighed, and he imagined her fussing with her red hair as she usually did when she was frustrated.

"You can't believe anything a vampire tells you. Didn't I already teach you that?"

"Well, you can teach me how to be dead now. I've been killed by now, surely."

"You're alive, little Z. I can feel it. I would know if you'd been killed. I promise."

He snorted. "The promises of imaginary friends mean nothing."

"Okay, then," she said. "I give up. Just promise me one thing."

"It depends what it is."

"Don't leave Shady Pines. It's safe there. They can't get to you there."

"I'm telling you they did."

"And I'm telling you you're not dead."

***

Chloe frowned, not sure what to make of the strange one-sided chat. She smiled when Zack's eyes seemed to focus suddenly. He moved his head slightly towards her, and she stroked his overlong dark hair back off of his face. "You're alive."

He smiled back wanly. "So I've been told."

CHAPTER NINETEEN

Being in hospital wasn't one of Zack's favourite things, but Chloe had brought him his gloves and she visited with food so he wouldn't need to depress himself with the standard hospital fare. He was glad to know he was only going to be in for the night this time. After she put the bag down in front of him, she sat down and promptly stood back up again.

"I should go."

"Stay," he said. "I'm still kind of fuzzy on what happened."

He could mention it because he'd lucked out and gotten a private room. He knew Bridget had tried to kill him, using Larry. He didn't really want to think about it if he was being honest, but he didn't want his rescuer to leave, either.

"Well," Chloe started, scratching at her head. "Bridget must have been working for a clan. It's the only reason she'd have for trying to turn you."

"She wasn't trying to kill me?"

Chloe's smile was small as she shook her head. "If she'd been aiming for that, she wouldn't have been able to order Larry to lay a hand on you."

He frowned. "I don't understand."

"You don't need to." She cleared her throat as her voice dried up. "There was no reason for her to kill you. She was definitely trying to turn you, and the chances are her clan will keep sending vampires to Shady Pines to try and take you. The good thing is, now they know what she was up to, the Council is coming up with increased plans to keep vampires out of town."

He took it in, wondering when it had become so normal to talk about vampires. He wondered if he'd even known about them before he'd lost his memory. Fear lingered at the back of his thoughts, but he refused to give it any wiggle room. This was one conversation he didn't want to space out on.

"So I'm safe here."

He remembered the weird talk he'd had with himself. It was strange. He didn't usually remember his dissociative episodes. The conversations with 'Audrey' had been different somehow. He wondered if there was a reason for that. "Can I ask you something?"

Her eyes widened for a second and then she nodded slowly.

"What happened the night they first came for me?" He wasn't sure she'd know, but he had to ask someone, and she was the only one he knew who might actually answer him.

"You mean, the night you lost your memories?"

She said it quietly as if she was afraid someone might overhear her.

"Yeah," he said. "Bridget told me vampires caused my

memory loss. I don't understand why they didn't turn me at that point. Something must have stopped them, I suppose. I feel like I must be missing something."

Chloe bit at her lip.

"You're not supposed to speak to me about it, right?" He knew there had to be something. Some reason he wasn't allowed to know. He sighed. Did he really want to do this? "I need to know."

"It's…" She took in a slow breath. "You weren't alone that night. The vampires left you for dead. They took your family. It seemed like they didn't want you or maybe something stopped them from finishing. No one could understand why, but that's what happened."

He let it sink in. "I had a family."

"Two brothers, one sister," Chloe told him.

"Audrey," he said, watching Chloe's face.

"You remember her?" Her voice softened.

He wasn't sure what to say. He knew what Audrey looked like, and he'd been having strange conversations with her inside his head for months. He felt his face flush. There was no way he was telling Chloe any of that. It made him sound insane. "I think I kind of do. I don't know how."

"Well, it's something," Chloe told him. "Maybe it means you'll get your other memories back."

"Maybe," he said, wondering if he really wanted them back. "I had a family."

She nodded. "I should go. Visiting hours are over, and I have to make a statement to the necromancer's Council."

"You weren't one of them," he said. "The necromancers

who were assigned to watch over me, I mean."

She shook her head. "I wasn't."

"Thanks for saving my life."

A ghost of a smile crossed her face. "It was nothing."

He watched her leave, his head reeling. He'd had a family. Vampires had taken them, but they'd left him behind. They'd taken everything that mattered to him: his family, his memories. He was nothing without them.

He remembered what Audrey had said to him, the one promise she'd wanted him to give her. He was not to leave Shady Pines.

He had an awful feeling he was going to have to break that promise.

Zack goes looking for his family in

SWEET OBLIVION

Read on for the first chapter

SHADY ARCADE BOOK TWO
SWEET OBLIVION

CHAPTER ONE

"She's never going to want to see me again," Larry complained in a whiny tone for the tenth time that morning. It was all he seemed capable of doing anymore.

Chloe rolled her eyes. Babysitting a lovesick vampire was the least of her problems. But it didn't matter how many times she told him he needed to snap out of it because his existence was at stake right now, he couldn't think of anything but Amira.

Is this what I've been like? She really hoped not. Losing Zack had hit her hard, but they'd been carving out a life together before he'd been left for dead and hit with a vampire induced bout of amnesia. Ten years didn't usually just get erased overnight.

"She saw you drink blood, Larry," Chloe told her friend as she checked over her handbook. "It usually takes a girl a week or two to get over that kind of thing."

He ran a hand through his hair and fell back in his seat dramatically. In spite of the irregular showering and unwashed clothes he was wearing, he looked like something out of a magazine. An aftershave ad featuring a hunky guy with a sullen stare…

Chloe snapped out of it. She had to stop looking at him like that. He was just her friend and she was sort of his guardian, for now at least. He wasn't a potential rebound, no matter how good he looked these days. Vampirism had agreed with him. That was all. She took a breath, and he was standing over her when she looked up again.

Shit, she thought. *Did he notice the way I was looking at him?*

"What are you…"

"You have to call her for me," he said, holding out his phone. "Please?"

"What makes you think she wants to talk to *me*?" Chloe had to ask. The girl had freaked, and that was putting it lightly. "It's only been a week, Larry. Give her time."

"I can't." He held the phone out until she took it.

She sighed. He held her gaze with his sad eyes until she relented and dialled Amira's number. The girl let her phone ring out. Chloe smiled wryly. "I'll try again later. Okay?"

He sighed and sank back into the couch as if he was liquid. "Later. Okay. Later."

She put the phone down and picked up the book. She'd found nothing to tell her what she was going to face for what she'd done. The Necromancer's Council had remained tight-lipped throughout her statement. She'd been told to take the week to train Larry and that they'd arrange a hearing. Her stomach was in knots. She could still see their blank expressions as she recounted the night she'd almost lost Zack for the second time. Her voice had been cracking, and it wasn't just because of the bruising Kenny's attack had left on her throat. The Elders had remained unemotional. She'd bitten back tears and tried to keep her face straight as she shook inside, terrified at what was going to happen to her. She'd killed a vampire. It wasn't something she'd ever thought she'd do. She shouldn't have needed to. Her abilities to command the dead should have avoided that kind of situation. That was going to be what they told her. Her excuses wouldn't matter.

She'd had one choice to stop Larry. Kill the vampire who'd commanded him to drink from Zack. She couldn't have countered Bridget's will with anything else. By the time she'd commanded Bridget to get Larry to stop, it would have been too late for Zack. With the added threat of Kenny in the room, she'd had no other choice. She couldn't let Zack die. And that was what was going to put her behind bars or wherever they actually sent necromancers who killed things.

"Try again?" Larry asked, hope in his mournful eyes.

He was like a kid, a big, blood-thirsty kid who'd be without a guardian soon enough. What was going to happen to him when she went away? She dreaded to think. If he wound up with someone like Kenny he'd turn out as badly as Bridget had. She didn't want that for him. It wasn't his fault some vampire had shown up and turned him. She sighed and picked her own phone out of her pocket. She'd been waiting for the call from the Council for what felt like forever. It was time to stop waiting around for her death sentence. She called Amira. The girl picked up cautiously after a few rings.

"Chloe?"

"It's me. How've you been?" She felt the air move as Larry darted to her side. He knelt down beside her, listening in on her conversation. It should have been weird, but she'd gotten used to his invasions of her personal space in the last week.

"Is that a trick question?" Amira sounded hurt.

"It's not. I… you saved my life."

"And you've been lying to me for who knows how long."

Chloe winced. "It's not… we're forbidden from telling humans. It's a law, it's not…"

"You knew Larry was… one of those *things*?" She sounded irritable.

Chloe watched Larry's face drop. "He was turned by a vampire recently. It wasn't his choice."

The pause on the line made her stomach twist. She didn't want to lose Amira as a friend, but she wasn't sure she was getting any say in the matter.

"I liked him." Amira sighed. "This is just… I can't even…" She sighed again.

"He's not dangerous," Chloe said.

"Tell that to Zack's neck," Amira said.

"Bridget used compulsion on him. She used it on you both. She's gone now."

"Compulsion? This just gets grosser," Amira told her. "What about Larry?"

"What about him?" She watched the hope start to return to his eyes.

"Can he use that? Like, on me? Oh my God. How do I know I even really wanted to go out with him? Maybe he just made me say yes. Maybe I never really wanted to kiss him!"

Chloe winced. "He didn't use it. He doesn't know how. Amira, I'm sorry I lied to you. I'm sorry you got mixed up in this mess."

"I don't know if sorry covers this," Amira said, pausing after she spoke. "Can you just tell Larry to stop calling me?"

Chloe watched him slope off to his room, the sound of the door closing softly behind him making her sigh. "I'll tell him."

ABOUT THE AUTHOR

Sharon Stevenson lives in Scotland with her husband. She spends her spare time creating entertaining fantasy worlds full of strange creatures and unconventional characters. The Amazon bestselling Gallows series follows twin demon trackers Shaun and Sarah Gallows through fictional Scottish towns as they come up against various supernatural threats, while their biggest problems are caused by their own personal demons. The Raised series is a magical take on zombies, set in Edinburgh and Las Vegas, and following the after death adventures of twenty-three-year-old Pete and his friends.

Want to keep up to date with Sharon's latest releases, receive three exclusive short stories, and find out about subscriber only offers and giveaways?

Just sign up here:
http://sharonstevensonauthor.com/newsletter

68041631R00126

Made in the USA
Charleston, SC
01 March 2017